W9-CEJ-981

CLOTHO
THE
FATE

READ ALL THE BOOKS IN THE GODDESS GIRLS SERIES

ATHENA THE BRAIN

PERSEPHONE THE PHONY

APHRODITE THE BEAUTY

ARTEMIS THE BRAVE

ATHENA THE WISE

APHRODITE THE DIVA

ARTEMIS THE LOYAL

MEDUSA THE MEAN

GODDESS GIRLS SUPER SPECIAL:
THE GIRL GAMES

PANDORA THE CURIOUS

PHEME THE GOSSIP

PERSEPHONE THE DARING

CASSANDRA THE LUCKY

ATHENA THE PROUD

IRIS THE COLORFUL

APHRODITE THE FAIR

MEDUSA THE RICH

AMPHITRITE THE BUBBLY

HESTIA THE INVISIBLE

ECHO THE COPYCAT

CALLIOPE THE MUSE

PALLAS THE PAL

NYX THE MYSTERIOUS

MEDEA THE ENCHANTRESS

CLOTHO THE FATE

Goddess Girls

CLOTHO THE FATE

JOAN HOLUB & SUZANNE WILLIAMS

Aladdin

NEW YORK LONDON TORONTO SYDNEY NEW DELHI

This book is a work of fiction. Any references to historical events, real people, or real places are used fictitiously. Other names, characters, places, and events are products of the author's imagination, and any resemblance to actual events or places or persons, living or dead, is entirely coincidental.

An imprint of Simon & Schuster Children's Publishing Division
1230 Avenue of the Americas, New York, New York 10020
First Aladdin hardcover edition December 2019

Also available in an Aladdin paperback edition.

For information about special discounts for bulk purchases, please contact Simon & Schuster Special Sales at 1-866-506-1949 or business@simonandschuster.com.
The Simon & Schuster Speakers Bureau can bring authors to your live event. For more information or to book an event contact the Simon & Schuster Speakers Bureau at 1-866-248-3049 or visit our website at www.simonspeakers.com.
Book designed by Karin Paprocki
The text of this book was set in Baskerville.
Manufactured in the United States of America 1019 FFG
2 4 6 8 10 9 7 5 3 1
Library of Congress Control Number 2019943156
ISBN 978-1-4814-7024-7 (hc)
ISBN 978-1-4814-7023-0 (pbk)
ISBN 978-1-4814-7025-4 (eBook)

CONTENTS

We love our amazing Goddess Girls readers!

Charlotte S. and Aurora S., Caitlin R., Hannah R., Emeline D., Katie B., Hannah B., Gaby A., Valeria C., Layla O., Beth S., Kim R., Abi C., Nicky V., Zoey R., Maddy W., Lori F., Michelle H. and Izabella D., Christine D-H., Olive Jean D., Eli Reuben D., Layla S., Ainsley W. and Isla W., McKenna W., Andrade Family, Shakarra D., Ivan S., Mackenzie S., Sidney B., Grey B., Calvin S., Tyler S., MiKayla S., Garrett S., Lauren S., Baby bump S., A. Anderson, G. Anderson, Cassy G., Olivia M., Amelia, Sloane G., Jeremy G., Alyssa B., Stephanie T., Ellis T., Micah F., Sarah M., Kira L., Kristen S., Barbara E., Emily E., Ace S., and Paul H.

—J. H. and S. W.

1

Spin, Measure, Snip!

THE THREE FATES ARRIVED AND QUICKLY SAT side by side on a fluffy cloud high in the star-filled night sky above Mount Olympus, the tallest mountain in Greece. They were sisters. Clotho was the youngest, at age eleven. Her long black hair had blue highlights. Twelve-year-old Lachesis's brown hair was streaked with purple. Red-haired Atropos was thirteen.

Out of nowhere, a white scroll made of glowing

mist appeared to float in the air alongside them, unrolling itself till it was about ten feet long. This was the Destiny List. It held the names of all the mortal babies born (or about to be born) today. Slowly the scroll began to weave and curl itself around and among the sisters.

Like all goddessgirls, the three Fates possessed a great magical talent. Theirs was the ability to predict events that would happen throughout the lifetime of each and every mortal on Earth! (Also known as their fate or destiny.)

However, this ability required a team effort. It only worked when the sisters met together, like now, each playing her particular role, and each following the rules that had been set for them by Zeus, the King of the Gods and Ruler of the Heavens. Clotho's sisters loved rules. Knowing exactly what was expected of them made them feel comfy and calm. However, sometimes the idea of *breaking* the rules seemed more exciting to Clotho. Because that meant something surprising could happen. Maybe something fun!

Zeus's Rule #1 dictated each of the Fates' individual jobs. Clotho's began when she leaned over and peered at a newborn mortal's name and accompanying short description at the top of the misty list. The first half of her job was to announce this information.

"Tantalus, a mortal Greek boy," she read aloud.

"Happy birthday, Tantalus," Lachesis and Atropos chanted. As their words faded, Tantalus's name and description vanished from the scroll. Each sister now had one additional, very specific duty to perform in celebration of his birth.

Clotho went first. The remaining (and super-important) half of her job was to spin his Thread of Fate. She grasped her special distaff, a three-foot-long stick with thick, fluffy sheep's wool wrapped around its top end. The wool resembled cotton candy, except it was beige instead of pink. She clamped one end of the stick between her knees, angling its woolly end to rest against her chest so it stood upright. As one of her hands began twisting raw wool off the distaff into a long thread, it fed onto the spool-like spindle that she dangled from her other hand and set to spinning like a top. *Spin!*

Once that process was in motion, it was Lachesis's turn to do her job. She reached over and pulled some of Clotho's newly spun thread from the spindle. Eyeing it carefully, she pinched her thumb and index finger to mark a place along the thread's

length. This indicated the length of time Tantalus would live. *Measure!*

"It is the destiny of all mortals to die one day, but Tantalus's thread is long," Lachesis commented, sounding happy about that.

Atropos leaned forward, nodding. "A sign of good fortune." The blades of her fancy silver scissors flashed. In an instant she cut the thread to the exact length Lachesis had indicated with her fingers. *Snip!*

Now each of the sisters solemnly grasped the cut length of thread. On the count of three they let go, their fingers releasing it at the exact same moment. Like a kite tail, the thread floated in a slow, serpentine motion up toward the heavens. As it rose, a few small dark spots appeared upon it here and there. These represented times of trouble or sadness that would occur during this mortal boy's life. However,

many small sparkles appeared along the thread too. These represented times of joy and celebration. The Fates could read the spots and sparkles and knew what each one meant.

"Looks like Tantalus will enjoy a mostly happy life," murmured Lachesis, sounding pleased.

Atropos nodded in satisfaction. "His parents will love him well."

Clotho smiled, watching the thread containing his fate rise ever upward. Soon they'd send the threads of other newborn mortals to follow it, floating into the sky beyond. Eventually each thread would rise so high that it would disappear somewhere among the stars.

"He'll have a nice home on Earth too," Clotho added. She sighed dreamily. If only she herself had a home! Instead, every night she and her sisters met at a different location to work. It was their nature to never need sleep, so during the day they each went wherever they liked and did what they pleased. Basically, the three Fates were nomads. Her sisters were fine with that. But to a girl like Clotho, who would have preferred having one place to call her own, a place she could always return to, their situation was not at all fun.

To her, Tantalus and other mortals like him who had homes of their own seemed super lucky! There were just so many drawbacks to always having to roam. For one thing, she loved animals and wanted a pet. But with the way they moved around so much, that would just be too hard. So, no pets for her. Instead she had recently started knitting *pretend* pets.

Her gaze fell upon two colorful finger-size animals peeking out of her pocket. The cuddly kitten and pink-eared bunny were actually finger puppets.

She'd knitted them and others (such as a pointy-nosed fox, floppy-eared dog, and sweet gray mouse) earlier that day. Over the past weeks, she'd made so many animal puppets that she didn't know what to do with them all.

Sometimes when she and her sisters arrived at a new place to work for the night, Clotho would arrange these little plush creatures around herself. It comforted her to see them, and was her way of pretending that each of their meeting places was a temporary home. "Nesting," her sisters called it, as if she were a bird making a cozy nest for herself.

An elbow nudged her ribs. "Ow!" yipped Clotho. She shot Lachesis a surprised look. Then she slid her index finger into the cuddly kitten puppet and, in a squeaky voice, made it pretend speak. "I mean, me-OW!" She giggled.

Her sisters rolled their eyes, grinning at her fondly. “What are you, three years old?” teased Atropos.

Clotho grinned back. “Maybe I’m just young at heart!” It was a phrase she’d read in a scrollbook one time: It meant that you liked playing and doing fun things no matter how old you got.

“C’mon. We’ve got a lot of NFs to get through,” said Lachesis, pointedly looking from Clotho to the Destiny List. (*NF* was short for “newborn fates.”) After Tantalus’s name had disappeared from the scroll, the name below it had moved up to the top. And new names were always being magically added at the bottom of the wispy scroll list, every time another mortal baby was about to be born. Therefore, the list was never-ending.

“Okay, sorry,” Clotho said. There was a time for work and a time for play, and right now it was work time! Quickly she stuffed the kitten puppet back into her pocket, then glanced at the new name at the top of the list. "Meleager, a mortal Greek prince," she announced.

"Happy birthday, Prince Meleager," chanted her two sisters.

As Clotho spun his length of thread, she wondered what kind of home Meleager would have. A castle, probably. *Hmm. What would* my *perfect home look like?* she mused.

It didn't have to be fancy. It should have three rooms, one for each sister. They wouldn't need beds, though, since they never slept. Some hangout space, work space, and a kitchen would be good. Although the Fates didn't need to eat any of the foods that mortals ate, they sometimes did. Because food could be yummy!

She imagined her own room and how she might decorate it. It would have a closet for clothes and some shelves for her puppets and yarn and stuff. If she had her own room, she could keep her things organized. It would mean no more packing up her belongings into her oversize travel bag every morning in order to lug it onward to someplace new.

Speaking of her belongings, just then the cloud she and her sisters were sitting on shape-shifted and shrank a little. This caused her bag to tip over and fall open. Her favorite pink knitting needles rolled out and were teetering on the edge of the cloud, about to fall. *Oh no!* Abandoning her spinning for just a sec, she made a grab for the needles. *Got 'em!* Quickly, she sat back up, temporarily tucking the knitting needles in her lap.

Then, realizing what she'd just done, her heart sank. She'd broken Zeus's Rule #2. That was: *Never interrupt the telling of a fate.* Such an interruption could mess up a mortal's whole life!

Desperately, Clotho spun faster, trying to make up for lost time. But in her haste she spun out a longer thread for Prince Meleager than she'd meant to. It was so long that it got tangled and knotted, making it appear to be shorter than it actually was. And much shorter than Tantalus's thread had been.

Luckily, her sisters didn't notice. They were busy chatting about whether the cloud they all sat on was nimbus or cumulus and wondering if it might bring rain before sunrise, causing them to have to relocate from a soggy perch.

Seconds later, Lachesis measured and Atropos snipped. After her silver scissors flashed, they all three released Meleager's thread. Her sisters began to speak in sad, soft voices, saying something about a log burning in a fireplace. And how Meleager's life would be short, ending once the log became ashes.

Warily, Clotho watched Prince Meleager's thread float upward. Instead of gliding smoothly like all the threads before it, it jerked along like an inch-worm. To her surprise, one of these jerks caused it to briefly tangle with Tantalus's thread before the two threads separated again and continued to rise. What did it mean? Had the two boys' fates somehow become entwined?

Meanwhile, her sisters' attention had shifted and they hadn't seemed to notice what was going on with the threads. Instead, their eyes were on the rescued knitting needles sitting in her lap.

"You should put those in your bag," Atropos

scolded. She could sometimes be as snippy as her scissors! "What if they rolled off your lap, tumbled down to Earth, and poked some poor mortal in the top of the head?"

"Yeah, Zeus would not be happy about that," added Lachesis mildly. She almost always spoke in a calm way many would describe as "measured."

Clotho nodded meekly and did as Lachesis suggested. Zeus might not have an actual rule against poking mortals in the top of the head, but it was likely he wouldn't appreciate her doing that. Still, the risk of those knitting needles falling was the least of her worries right now. Meleager's too-long, tangled, knotted thread was far more problematic. Had she accidentally spun the mortal prince's life out longer than it was meant to be? Had that changed his destiny? Maybe Tantalus's, too?

The Fates' job was to set every mortal's destiny in motion. They were knot—er, *not*—supposed to interfere with that destiny.

Her sisters hadn't seemed to notice her mistake, but had Zeus? Clotho hunched her shoulders, her brown eyes nervously darting around the sky as she tucked the pink needles away in her bag and set it upright again. As King of the Gods and Ruler of the Heavens, Zeus was a mega-powerful guy (with a mega-powerful temper to match!). Still, as far as she knew, he couldn't see everything that went on everywhere all the time. At least she hoped not. She really didn't want him mad at her and her sisters. He might smite them with a white-hot thunderbolt or something! Fingers crossed he'd never find out about her mistake.

"Hello?" Lachesis nudged her again and nodded

toward the mist list. "Honestly, where is your head tonight? We need to get a move on."

Clotho knew she should admit to her sisters what had just happened. And she didn't exactly decide *not* to. It was only that the moment had passed. And it simply became easier not to mention her rule-break mistake than to admit it and stir up trouble.

As she read the next name on the list, she relaxed. No thunderbolts in sight. It looked like everything would be okay. *Phew!* That was a close call. She did her best to convince herself that messing up Meleager's thread wouldn't change anything. That she'd escaped trouble. Because that was what she *wanted* to believe.

Though she and her sisters could read the destinies of others, they couldn't even begin to guess their own. So right then, Clotho had no way of

knowing that a mere twelve years from this very date, both of the mortal boys whose threads she'd just spun would bring her trouble. Mighty Trouble, with a capital *M* as in Meleager and a capital *T* as in Tantalus.

2 Chariot Mail

(Twelve years later)

SO IT CAME TO BE THAT ONE SATURDAY EXACTLY twelve years later, trouble began. By now Clotho had forgotten all about her Meleager thread mistake. Despite the passing of time, she and her sisters still looked and felt the same ages they had always been and would always be. Unlike mortals, they would never grow old.

It was very early morning, and the three Fates had been working together through the dark night for almost eight hours by now, sitting side by side upon a strong branch high in an enormous oak tree in the land of Colchis along the Black Sea. A magnificent cape called the Golden Fleece, made from the wool of a rare and famous ram, had once hung on this very branch. That is, until an enchantress named Medea and an Argonaut named Jason had stolen it away.

Achoo! A puff of green smoke drifted up to them.

"Zeus bless you," Clotho politely called down to the humongous, sneezy serpent that lurked on the ground below. It made a grumbly, rumbly sound in reply and shuffled around the trunk of the tree. It had once guarded the fleece (unsuccessfully, since it had been stolen!). Although the fleece was gone, the serpent still patrolled the grove day in and day out.

Clotho read the name currently at the top of the Destiny List, then spun out a thread for a mortal girl. *Spin!*

Measure! Lachesis marked the thread to the correct length for the girl.

Snip! Seconds after Atropos cut the thread and the three sisters released it to rise above them, Clotho glanced eastward. Eos, the goddessgirl of the dawn, had just appeared on the far horizon to paint the waning night sky with soft colors of pink and orange. The sun peeked out, and the misty list disappeared. *Poof!* Another night's work had come to an end for the Fates.

"It's another new day," said Clotho. During the night she and her sisters had set in motion the destinies of hundreds of newborn mortals. Pleased, she tucked her distaff and spindle into her travel bag.

"Time for mortals to begin waking up," Lachesis murmured.

Atropos cocked her head. "I wonder what it's like to sleep."

"Dreamy?" joked Clotho, giggling. She thought her reply was funny, but her sisters only smiled slightly.

"Let's meet on the constellation Orion tonight," suggested Atropos. "Since it has three stars on its belt, there'll be one for each of us to sit on."

"Stars are always a good choice," Lachesis agreed. "We'll have bright light to work by."

The Fates took turns choosing where they'd work each night. Lachesis had chosen the oak tree tonight. After Atropos's Orion pick, Clotho's turn would come again. That was the way it went, night after night. Her sisters never seemed to grow tired of the constant moving from place to place the way she did. She was the only one who longed for a home where they could all three just stay put!

"So where are you guys off to for the day?" Lachesis asked. Standing up on their wide, long branch, she reached for her bag of belongings. The girls had each hung their bags on the tree's smaller branches earlier that night. "I'm heading to a conference in Rome to discuss the nature of measurement. For instance, you wouldn't use the same method to measure a length of thread as you would to measure things like courage, creativity, and strength."

"No indeed." Atropos tilted her face up. "I'm thinking I'll fly high until I find some snow and frost to cut into snowflakes that'll flurry down to Earth. Just for fun. Of course, that'll dull my scissors, but

I'll sharpen and oil them before we work tonight."

"Sounds good. Your plans and meeting at the constellation, I mean," Clotho said. She reached up to a smaller branch to gather the finger-puppet friends she had set out along it before starting to work.

"So what'll you get up to today? Planning to knit more dogs, cats, kittens, and caboodles?" teased Atropos, as Clotho tucked all but two of the little puppets into her travel bag.

Clotho slipped the remaining two—a green dragon and a striped orange cat—onto two of her fingers. "*Rrroar!* Are caboodles something to eat? I'm hungry!" she made the green serpent puppet say, flexing her finger.

"*ROARRR!*" echoed the real serpent below them, sending a huge puff of green smoke floating up. The girls coughed, waving it away.

Startled, Clotho dropped the serpent puppet. It fell down, down, down, where the real serpent caught it. It sniffed it somewhat suspiciously at first, then stuck it on one claw. Wiggling the claw, it grinned at the puppet, showing pointy, white, scary-looking teeth.

"He thinks he's found a friend," whispered Lachesis.

"That is hilarious," snickered Atropos.

Clotho leaned down and wiggled the orange cat, which had tiny whiskers and a pink nose, so the serpent could see it. Speaking in a high, sweet kitty voice, she called to the green beast, "Maybe I'll knit a little serpent family for you. Wouldn't that be *purr*-fect?"

The serpent's eyes lit up. It nodded eagerly.

Her sisters giggled in surprise to see such a big bad serpent's heart melting over a teeny puppet friend. He was lonely, Clotho realized. And her puppet made him feel less so.

Hmm. She knew how he felt. She often felt lonely too. Of course, she was lucky to have two sisters that were also her good friends. Still, she longed to make new friends, too. To hang out with girls who wouldn't think they had the right to tell her what to do just because she was the youngest, and who didn't *always* talk about the same ol' stuff. Sometimes she'd like to talk about other kinds of things, things that didn't really interest her sisters, like maybe sports or pets or knitting puppets.

Clotho flicked the cat puppet into her bag. Then she poked around inside it to search for the colored yarn she'd need to knit more serpents. "Looks like I'll need more green yarn. Also more wool for tonight's fate-spinning."

Just then a loud whooshing sound reached her ears. Hermes, the messenger of the gods, came zooming across the sky toward them in a silver chariot piled high with letterscrolls and packages. Upon reaching the girls, he put his chariot on autopilot. It began to circle alongside their branch, powered by a pair of mighty white wings that flapped on the chariot's sides.

"Delivery!" With that announcement, Hermes plunged headlong into the mound of scrolls to search for something.

"Delivery?" Clotho echoed in surprise. For some reason his announcement caused her sisters to exchange nervous looks. What was up with that?

Lachesis turned to Clotho. "Maybe you should get going to look for that yarn and wool you need." Atropos nodded in agreement. It almost seemed like her sisters were in a hurry to get rid of her.

"I'm thinking I might drop some of my finger puppets off at the homes of lonely mortals down in Greece," Clotho mumbled, her curious gaze on Hermes. "And maybe take a bunch to the parents of some newborn mortals too. They could do finger-puppet shows to entertain their newborns when they cry."

At this, her sisters seemed to temporarily forget about Hermes. When they eyed her, she hunched her shoulders. She knew what was coming. And sure enough . . .

"That would be a violation of Zeus's Rule Number Three," Atropos warned her.

"I know, I know. He doesn't want us mingling with mortals," said Clotho. "I'll just drop them off secretly. Sneak in; sneak out. No will even know I was ever there."

Before either of her sisters could further object to her plan, Hermes yelled, "Aha! Found it." He pulled out a box full of letterscrolls and straightened, triumph gleaming in his eyes. "Incoming!" he called, tossing the box down to them.

Thump! It landed closest to Clotho on the thick tree branch she and her sisters stood upon. The box teetered for a moment and the serpent below eyed it, letting out a blast of fire. Luckily, she managed to rescue the box before it could fall into the creature's claws or jaws.

"Give me that!" her sisters both called out. Clotho didn't listen. Lifting the lid, she eyed the letterscrolls in the box quizzically. All were addressed to *The Fates*.

A feeling of delight rose up in her. "Mail? For us? I can't believe it. We *never* get mail!" Because they didn't have a home with a mailing address, of course! *Grr.*

"Huh?" said Hermes. "Yes, you do. Your sisters pick it up at my office in the Immortal Marketplace once a week."

Speaking to Lachesis and Atropos, he added, "I know you would've come for it soon. But I happened to see you here as I was passing by, so I decided to save you a trip. Hey, hold on. Might have more for you in here somewhere."

As he dove into the pile of packages and scrolls in the back of his chariot again, Clotho frowned at her sisters. "We get mail? How come you never told me? That's not fair!"

"Wait!" said Lachesis, as Clotho unrolled a letter-scroll.

"Don't!" said Atropos.

Before they could stop her, Clotho began reading the letterscroll. Its contents caused her to frown. Putting it aside, she read a second one. And then, with growing dismay, a third. All were from mortals—unhappy, complaining mortals.

"These letterscrolls are mean!" she exclaimed to her sisters. She read the worst parts of the three aloud:

"Fates, you stink! I wanted to be a teacher, but you made it my destiny to become a doctor. One who faints at the sight of blood!"

"Hey, you bossy Fates, I wanted to travel around the world. But no, you made me live my whole life in the same city. So boring. Thanks for nothing!"

"Dear FinkFates, I'm so mad at you. You let my granny die. You are villains!"

A terrible feeling of hurt squeezed Clotho's heart. Because who wanted to be considered a villain? Not her! And she wasn't. Her sisters weren't either. She looked at them with sorrowful eyes. "Mortals don't like us?"

"They fear your power," Hermes replied before her sisters could open their mouths. His chariot was now hovering only a few feet from them. "They don't like you bossing them around and deciding their destinies."

Clotho glared at Hermes. "We *don't* boss them around. It's the Destiny List and the Threads of Fate that together decide who they'll be and what they'll do. And how long they'll live, too. We just set things in motion." She angrily squeezed the letterscrolls she still clutched, crumpling them. "They should be grateful to us for doing that, not mad at us."

Looking a little nervous, Hermes held up his hands, palms facing out. "Hey, don't blame the messenger. I didn't *write* those letterscrolls, remember? I just delivered them."

Lachesis spread her hands. "See? This is why we've always picked up the mail in secret and hidden these letters from you," she told Clotho. "We knew they'd upset you."

Clotho's eyebrows rose and so did her voice. "You mean we've gotten mean letters like these before?"

Lachesis nodded. "Lots of 'em."

"Sadly, mortals don't get that we don't *decide* their fates. We just set them in motion, like you said, Clotho," added Atropos. "If we didn't do our job each night, their lives would have no plan. They'd be aimless!"

"We should write them all back and tell them that," urged Clotho.

Lachesis shook her head, her dark brown hair flickering with purple highlights as it swung at her shoulders. "Rule Number Three, remember? No mingling with mortals. And exchanging letters would be mingling."

"It's not fair that we can't explain," grumbled Clotho.

"Zeus makes rules for a reason," Atropos reminded her sharply.

"But what's the reason for this one?" asked Clotho. "I don't get it."

Lachesis shrugged. "Who knows? Anyway, you do understand that by keeping the mortals' letter-scrolls from you, we were only trying to protect you from their unkind words. Right, little sis?"

Mm-hm. Treat her like a baby, her sister meant. Even though Clotho's feelings were both hurt and confused, she nodded reluctantly. "So mortals have always feared us?" When her sisters didn't reply, she took that for a yes.

"Um . . . what kind of animals are you going to knit in your free time today?" asked Lachesis. She was obviously trying to lighten things up by changing the subject.

"I don't know," Clotho said with a sigh. She wasn't sure what hurt more: the mean letters themselves, or the fact that her sisters had hidden them from her. They may have believed they were protecting her, but their secretiveness only made her feel left out.

Hermes paused in the act of searching through his packages to gaze down at Clotho in surprise. "You mean you don't know what your *own* fate will be today? I thought the Fates knew everything."

"Actually, we can't even predict in advance where

we'll be working from one night to the next," blurted Clotho. Slyly she added, "If we had a home, that would be easy, of course."

"Uh-oh, here we go again," muttered Atropos, rolling her eyes.

Hermes' head popped up from his dive into the packages to nod so hard at them that the small wings on the cap he wore began to flap, causing it to lift off his head. "That would be mega-awesome," he said, snatching the cap and putting it back on securely. "If you had a permanent address, I could deliver your mail directly to you all the time." Efficiently, he continued to toss down additional letterscrolls addressed to them as he discovered more.

Even though she wasn't sure she and her sisters would want to *read* that mail if it only contained letter-scrolls as nasty and complaining as the few she'd just read, Clotho felt a spurt of triumph. She turned to her sisters. "See? Even Hermes agrees we need a home."

Atropos folded her arms. "A home base would only lead to trouble," she said stubbornly. "If mortals always knew where to find us, they wouldn't just *send* us grumpy letters. They'd come visit to complain to us *in person*."

"Yeah, how fun would that be? Not at all!" said Lachesis, shaking her head.

Hmm. Her sisters had a point. And yet . . .

"I still think we should do something to convince them we're not meanies. To earn their respect," Clotho replied. "Besides, I don't agree that writing back to them would be mingling. We need to explain what we do for them and how important it is. And anyway, I mean, I love you guys, but a chance to make some other friends, even as pen pals, might be nice too."

Her sisters looked aghast. "You can't have mortal friends!" they exclaimed in unison.

"Yeah, yeah. Zeus's rule," said Clotho, feeling frustrated. Rule #3 was one rule she could do without!

"It's really not a good idea," Lachesis said gently.

Thunk! Hermes tossed out one last letterscroll, which Atropos caught.

"That's all for now!" he called out cheerily.

Clotho had no desire to read any more of those mean letterscrolls. Her sisters had stuffed them in their bags and were ignoring them too, at least for now. Frustrated and feeling antsy, she grabbed her bulky travel bag. "I'm off to go find more wool. And some green yarn."

Overhearing, Hermes called down to her as he rearranged the packages left in his chariot. "Try the

Immortal Marketplace. There's a shop there called Arachne's Sewing Supplies. It closed a while back, but I think it still has all its remaining stock of yarn and wool. Now that the owner's gone, I'm sure no one would mind if you took some."

With that he swung back into the driver's seat, and with a flap of mighty white wings, his chariot whisked him away. His final words floated back to them. "A new place called Game On! is opening across the atrium from the shop, so just follow the crowds going to its grand opening."

"Thanks! I'll check it out!" Clotho called after him.

"Uh, no you won't," Atropos said sharply.

Lachesis nodded in agreement. "The Immortal Marketplace is off-limits. It's not just immortals who shop there. Mortals do too."

"If they notice you and figure out you're a Fate,

they'll either complain about their destinies or ask you to grant favors. Long life, more toys, new boyfriends or girlfriends, chocolate, jewels, all kinds of things we can't and shouldn't deliver," said Atropos.

"Yeah," said Lachesis. "One time, this eight-year-old boy wrote to us for a real sword! And another time, a little girl begged us to turn her feet into duck feet."

Clotho planted her fists on both sides of her waist. "But you both go to the IM."

"Only to get mail," said Atropos. "We go early before most shoppers arrive, keep our heads down, and never speak to any mortals there."

"So that's what I'll do too. Zip into the IM, get what I need at that sewing shop, and zip back out," Clotho argued. "Then I'll find a rainbow somewhere to perch on to work on my knitting."

"Let's put your idea to a vote," suggested Atropos.

"I vote no," both sisters said at the same time. As usual, they stuck together. Two against one. Since Clotho was the one, her vote made no difference. At times like this, she really wished she were not a Fate. Not part of a team. Able to make her own choices. Instead she always had to abide by her older sisters' wishes. Not to mention Zeus's unfair rules. *Argh!*

3

The Immortal Marketplace

CLOTHO HEFTED HER TRAVEL BAG AND PULLED its straps over one shoulder, then bent at the waist to call down to the serpent. "Yoo-hoo! As soon as I have your little green puppet family ready, I'll come back and drop them off, okay?"

Snorts sounded and green puffs floated up to the three sisters through the branches of the tree they stood in. Clotho figured that meant "Great!" in serpent lingo.

"Where are you going?" Atropos asked her, sounding suspicious.

"I need wool for tonight's work, remember?" Clotho replied. "There won't be any lying around on Orion. I mean, it's not like sheep graze on constellations. I'm sure there's a sheep herd around here somewhere. I'll find one and do a little shearing. I'll also have to spin some yarn and dye it green to make the serpent family. Busy, busy."

"Well, that's okay, then. See you tonight," said Lachesis.

Clotho saluted her sisters like they were pirate ship captains. "Aye, aye."

"No dallying," Atropos cautioned. "Be at Orion's Belt before nightfall."

"I know, I know," Clotho grumped. Honestly! Were her sisters ever going to stop treating her like a child? They weren't even that much older than her! Swallowing her frustration, she said, "I'll set my sandals to *warp* speed to make sure I get there on time. Ha-ha! Get it?"

When Lachesis and Atropos looked at her blankly, she explained. "Warp. You know, as in warp and weft." Those were terms for the two kinds of directional threads that crossed on a loom to weave fabric. Actually the terms had nothing to do with speed. "Warp speed" referred to a scientifically impossible kind of travel. If warp speed were truly possible, she'd be able to distort space and time to move faster than the speed of light. How cool would that be!

Her sandals, which she'd knitted from brightly colored yarn, weren't anywhere near that fast.

However, they *were* magical and would fly her any-where she wanted to go. Quickly, she chanted to them:

"Magic sandals,
Fly with speed
To find some sheep
With the wool I need."

At her words, the fist-size fluffy pom-poms, one atop each of her sandals, began to spin around like whirlybirds. The sandals lifted her off the branch and whisked her up and away. Soon green farm fields, turquoise seas, and cityscapes were passing far below in a blur of jeweled colors. A brisk wind whipped through her sleek black hair, turning her ears pink with cold.

Halfway between the Earth and Mount Olympus, the high-ceilinged crystal roof of the Immortal Marketplace came into view. She eyed it curiously. Unlike her sisters, she'd never been inside it.

When a sudden feeling of warmth fell upon her, she glanced up. A golden chariot was racing across the sky overhead carrying a huge ball of golden flame. The driver, Helios the sun god, waved to her. "Thanks for the sunshine!" Clotho called up to him, waving back.

Oops! Her waving jostled the bag she carried over one shoulder. She felt something fall from it. Alarmed, she looked down and watched her distaff tumble toward the IM. She dipped lower, zooming after it.

Minutes later, her magic sandals touched down on a wide slab of fancy marble tiles outside the IM entrance where she thought the distaff had landed.

She looked around for it, heart pounding. Finally, she spotted it lying by the IM's front doors. *Phew!*

She scurried over to pick it up. While stowing it in her bag, she caught sight of a carousel through those double glass doors. One with all kinds of exotic animals to ride. How mega-cool was that? If only she could go inside for a closer look. She reached for the doors but then dropped her hand. Her sisters had warned her to stay out of the IM. Someone might recognize her as a Fate. Or she might accidentally talk to some mortals. That would be breaking the rules.

Oof! As she backed away, she suddenly bumped into someone. She whirled around to see a girl about her age with fire-gold hair and almond-shaped brown eyes. She was carrying a bunch of boxes and bags piled high in her arms and heading for the Marketplace doors.

"Oh no!" wailed the girl, stumbling back from the force of Clotho's jostle. Some of the boxes and bags she'd been carrying slid sideways and toppled to the ground.

"Sorry!" said Clotho, picking them up.

"Thanks," replied the girl. Arms full, she didn't move to take her packages, and only stood uncertainly before the doors, probably wondering how she was going to open one to get through. "Um . . . could you . . . ?" She looked around her mound of stuff at Clotho, a question in her eyes.

"Oh sure. Need some help?" Clotho asked politely. Immediately, she wanted to call back her words. Because she'd just noticed that this girl's skin did not sparkle the way an immortal's skin would. Therefore she must be a mortal. And naturally, Clotho didn't want to break Zeus's rule about not mingling with mortals.

(Even if it was a dumb rule, in her humble opinion.) Then again, it was simply good manners to heed this girl's plea for help. Right? Surely Zeus wouldn't want her to be rude. She'd heard he was big on hospitality.

The girl nodded. "Yes, please."

Her mind made up, Clotho pulled one of the doors open. The girl slipped through, packages tottering. One of the boxes the girl was carrying bumped the door frame. Her load tipped to one side. *Uh-oh!* Clotho leaped forward and grabbed two burlap sacks that appeared to be filled with flour before they could fall.

"Could you bring those for me, please? Thanks," the girl called over her shoulder. Without waiting for Clotho to hand back the sacks, she sped up, moving down the wide hallway of the IM. She seemed to assume that Clotho would follow.

And Clotho did. “Wait! Your stuff!” As she chased after the girl, she glanced ahead. The IM was enormous, with rows and rows of shops separated by tall, ornate columns. Quickly, they came even with the carousel. It was *sooo* amazing. Clotho studied the wooden animals on the revolving platform, thinking maybe she’d knit some finger puppets to match them. How cool would that be?

The mortal girl stopped in front of a shop across from the carousel. The sign over its door read: ORACLE-O BAKERY AND SCROLLBOOKS. A smaller sign hanging from the doorknob read: CLOSED.

“Would you mind opening this door for me too?” called the girl.

Still gripping the flour sacks and shouldering her travel bag, Clotho dashed over and did as asked.

The girl darted into the shop, smiling back at her.

"I'm Cassandra, by the way. I suppose you're here for the grand opening of Game On!—that new gaming store opening up here in the IM today?"

"Oh, um, no. I heard about it, though," said Clotho, recalling what Hermes had said. *Ack!* What was she doing talking to this mortal girl? She was trying to follow the rules and hadn't meant to chat with any mortals, but what was she supposed to do? Not help? Not answer? Just throw the girl's stuff through the door and run away? No! Surely Zeus wouldn't want her to purposely not respond when spoken to. Besides, the thrill of hanging out with a girl her own age even for a few minutes was hard to resist. She rarely got the chance to talk with anyone but her sisters.

She dropped her travel bag just inside the door, then followed Cassandra over to the counter, where they set everything else down. Clotho spun around and headed straight back for the door. She intended to leave right away. She really did. But then she got a whiff of the air around her. This was the best-smelling room she'd ever been in! She sniffed at the air greedily, then breathed out a happy sigh. "What smells so good?"

"Everything!" said Cassandra, laughing merrily. "This is my family's bakery. My mom's, brother's, sister's, and mine, I mean. We made all the refreshments for the Game On! event today. You really should go. The party snacks will be dee-licious, if I do say so myself. Sweets, little sandwiches, all kinds of stuff."

Moving past Clotho, Cassandra flipped the sign on the bakery door from CLOSED to OPEN. Then she moved back to the counter and began pulling things from the boxes and sacks they'd brought in.

In addition to the flour, there were things like sugar, butter, eggs, and papyrus bags.

Clotho stood glancing around, unable to resist a peek at the scrumptious goodies attractively displayed on shelves and small tables throughout the shop. Doughnuts, tarts, cookies of all kinds, chocolates, and more. She saw the ovens where everything was baked too, and an opening on one wall that led to a book-scroll store. Finally, remembering that she shouldn't be here, she moved in the direction of the door.

Again Cassandra's voice stopped her. "Would you mind?" The girl held a stack of papyrus bags with the store logo on them out to Clotho. "These go on that shelf over there. They're for customers to fill with random goodies."

Clotho knew she should leave. Right now. But her feet seemed to have other ideas. They turned and moved her back toward the counter. Taking the stack, she set the bags neatly on the shelf Cassandra had indicated. Before she knew it, she was busily helping to stow more items in bins or on shelves.

"So anyway, we used up all our supplies making snacks for the Game On! grand opening I was telling you about," Cassandra went on. "I'm minding the shop alone this morning while the rest of my family is all out shopping for even more supplies to restock. Today we're going to be baking the goodies for Zeus's birthday party tomorrow here in the IM. We'll need plenty because that big guy has a *huge* sweet tooth!"

Clotho smiled. She loved how organized everything was in here. She drew in another deep breath of delicious smells. Cinnamon. Lemon. Chocolate. *Mmm.* Time to go.

"Hey, why don't you fill one of those bags with some goodies for yourself? Pick out anything you like," Cassandra offered, ducking down behind the shop's long counter to stow a bag of sugar away. "For free. A thank-you gift for helping me."

Just as the Fates did not need to sleep, the only foods they really needed to eat or drink were nectar and ambrosia. Those kept them immortal, though they didn't cause their skin to shimmer as they did with other goddesses and gods.

However, like Zeus, Clotho had a sweet tooth for sure, so Cassandra didn't have to offer twice. "Okay, thanks," she replied, picking up one of the shop's papyrus bags. Immediately her eyes went to some baskets of cookies on the main counter.

Popping back up from behind the counter just then, Cassandra noticed the direction of her gaze.

"Those are Oracle-O cookies. There's a prophecy or fortune tucked inside each of them. My brother, Helenus, puts them in. Sometimes he writes the prophecies on slips of papyrus. Other times he just whispers them into the cookie, which gives the cookie the ability to speak that prophecy later to whoever eats it."

"Why is one of the baskets labeled *Opposite* Oracle-Os?" Clotho asked, curious.

Cassandra grinned. "Long story short, I tell prophecies too. But no one believes them, even though they actually will come true. So to trick everyone into believing them, I write the *opposite* of what I know to be a true prophecy in my fortunes."

"Oh, I get it," said Clotho, unable to cut short this forbidden conversation. "So you write a lie. And then whoever gets the fortune believes the opposite of that lie. And that opposite is actually the truth."

Erg! What was she doing? Carrying on a conversation with a mortal, that's what! Breaking Zeus's rule!

"Exactly!" said Cassandra, looking pleased that Clotho had caught on to her explanation.

Quickly Clotho nabbed one of each kind of Oracle-O cookie. Cassandra smiled at her choices. If only she could tell this mortal girl something about herself. Would Cassandra feel the same way about the Fates as those complaint-letterscroll-writing mortals felt, though? Would she look at Clotho in fear or yell at her? She wasn't sure. So confiding her identity to this mortal was probably not a good idea. Too bad, because she and Cassandra had fortune-telling in common. It would have been fun to talk about prophecies and their pitfalls.

With a sigh, Clotho turned and took a step toward

the exit. At the same time, the little bell on the store's front door tinkled, and a girl holding several large papyrus scrolls came in. She had blue eyes and long golden hair and wore a shimmery pink chiton.

Clotho stopped in her tracks. She couldn't help staring. The girl was that beautiful! She had seen enough statues and painted friezes around Mount Olympus to recognize this famous goddessgirl right away.

"Hi, Aphrodite. Whatcha got there?" Cassandra greeted the girl, confirming what Clotho had already guessed. That this was the goddessgirl of love and beauty, a student at Mount Olympus Academy. She looked about twelve years old, and way more amazing in real life than as a statue or painting!

"Posters advertising the Game On! grand opening today. Mind if I hang one in your shop window?" Aphrodite asked. "Ares is spreading them around the IM and I offered to help. He's pretty gung ho about the new gaming shop, as you can imagine."

"The godboy of war? Excited about what's rumored to be some kind of indoor war game? What a surprise!" said Cassandra. The two girls laughed. "And yes, you can put up the poster," Cassandra added.

Aphrodite began affixing the poster to the inside of the shop's glass door so it faced out toward the atrium. Momentarily blocked from leaving, Clotho watched her out of the corner of her eye. As Aphrodite worked, she also glanced at Clotho, but Clotho pretended not to notice. Instead, she busily checked out the bakery goods on various shelves and cutely decorated tables. Now and then she added more goodies to her bag. As soon as Aphrodite left, she would go too, she promised herself.

Minutes later, Aphrodite finished her task and moved to the counter to chat with Cassandra. Clotho picked up her travel bag and headed for the door. Immediately, its bell tinkled again and a mortal girl entered, blocking the exit once more. She started asking questions the minute she saw Cassandra putting away supplies. "Hey, what's with all the new ingredients? Did you use up what you already had on hand baking stuff for the Game On! grand opening? So you went and got more? Because Zeus's birthday is coming up? Is your shop going to cater his party?"

"Yes to all," Cassandra replied, her eyes twinkling.

Just then, the question-asking girl noticed Clotho. "Hey, I'm Pandora. What's your name?"

"Clotho," she replied before she could think

better of it. *Argh!* She hunched her shoulders. Why hadn't she made up a fake name? She shouldn't get chummy with these girls, she reminded herself. But the curious Pandora's rapid-fire questions had set her head spinning. Fittingly, the curious girl's bangs were curled in the shape of question marks.

When none of the girls in the bakery reacted to her big reveal, Clotho straightened. They hadn't recognized her name! She probably shouldn't be surprised. Although most everyone on Earth and Mount Olympus knew of the three Fates, they usually considered them a group, not individuals with names (and personalities) of their own. This thought was kind of depressing, actually. She and her sisters were each quite different.

If these girls found out who she really was, however, there could be trouble. Her secret identity as a

Fate was best kept just that—secret. Unfortunately, Pandora opened her mouth to ask another nosy question. "Who?"

Panicking, Clotho murmured, "Sorry. Lots to do. Gotta get a move on." She ducked her head, darted away, and grabbed a star-shaped cookie from one of the bins. Just in case Pandora decided to follow her, she stuffed the whole thing in her mouth so she'd be unable to respond to any further questions the girl might ask. *Crunch!*

Jingle-jangle! Saved by the cookie *and* the bell! Well, not quite, since the door was still blocked. Pandora moved away from it as three more goddess-girls trooped into the shop. Still chewing, Clotho studied the new arrivals, recognizing them right off.

First came Persephone, the goddessgirl of growing things, whose long wavy red hair had flowers twined in it. Next was Artemis, the black-haired goddessgirl of the hunt, who carried a quiver of arrows and a bow slung over one shoulder. And finally the brown-haired, superbrainy Athena—Zeus's daughter. Not only was her dad the King of the Gods and Ruler of the Heavens, he was also the principal of Mount Olympus Academy. And as everybody knew, these three girls, along with Aphrodite, were BFFs and the most popular goddessgirls at that school!

Immediately, Pandora turned her questions on *them*, thank godness! "Hey! What are you doing here, Persephone? Weren't you going home with your mom this weekend?"

At the word "home," Clotho's ears perked up. She had thought all these goddessgirls lived in dorms at MOA. (How she envied them having places to call their own where they could keep their stuff organized!) What would she say if they asked her where *she* lived? she wondered. She wouldn't want to lie, but she also wouldn't want to admit the truth. That she was homeless. If she told them that, it might lead to other questions she couldn't answer without revealing the fact that she was one of the unpopular Fates.

Pandora didn't even give Persephone a chance to respond before she began asking Athena questions about her dad's forthcoming birthday party. Meanwhile, everyone else began to chat with one another. Clotho shifted the straps of her bag higher on her shoulder and eyed the door. As stealthily as possible, she edged toward it. Now that everyone was so busy chatting, maybe she could finally slip out of the shop unnoticed. Halfway there, however, her eye fell on a display of animal-shaped cookies and she paused. *Hmm.*

No one was looking her way. So, just for fun, she randomly plucked out some of her knitted animal finger puppets—a fuzzy black-footed lamb, a pink round-belly corkscrew-tail pig, and a half dozen more. Darting glances at the other girls to be sure they weren't looking her way, she quickly set the little puppets on the display, scattered attractively among the cookies. They added a nice, quirky, cute touch. Perfect!

"So, are you going home?" Pandora asked Persephone once more.

"Yeah, but just to sleep. I'll be, um, hanging here at the IM a lot during the daytime," Persephone told her.

"But I thought you said you were going to be doing some work in the Underworld," Aphrodite put in.

"Hades asked Persephone to help him on a project," Athena informed Pandora, waggling her eyebrows. "But she's being all mysterious and won't say what kind of project exactly."

"Huh?" Pandora began, looking more curious than ever.

Clotho was curious as well. Her ears had perked up at the mention of the Underworld, which was ruled by the godboy Hades. It was where mortals went after they'd died and crossed the River Styx. She and her sisters knew a lot about it because of their work with the Destiny List. Lachesis especially, since she was in charge of measuring out the lengths of mortal lives.

Persephone grinned at them all, definitely looking mysterious. "Sorry. For now, it's a secret."

Jingle-jangle! Another girl's head poked in through

the doorway. "Secret?" she echoed. "Did someone say 'secret'?" This new girl had apparently been listening at the bakery door, and now she pushed it open and stepped inside. She had short, spiky orange hair and a pair of small orange wings that flapped gently at her back. With her entry there were now eight girls total in the shop. The place was getting crowded!

Persephone smiled good-naturedly at the orange-haired girl. "Leave it to you to sniff out breaking news, Pheme."

So this was Pheme, the goddessgirl of gossip. Made sense that she'd keep her ears open for interesting tidbits of information she could pass around. Especially info about immortals, since mortals avidly read *Teen Scrollazine* for news of what they were up to.

Pheme licked her orange-glossed lips as if actually hungry for whatever news Persephone was willing to share. With a grin, she said, "Hey, my column in *Teen Scrollazine* doesn't write itself, you know. I need scoop. C'mon. Spill." The words puffed in the air in cloud letters that rose above her for everyone to read before later fading away.

Now Persephone looked a little nervous, likely wary of Pheme's famed ability to trick people into giving out information they'd vowed to keep to themselves. "Uh . . ."

Luckily Artemis butted in, to Persephone's obvious relief. "You want secrets? I've got one. I helped design the first game in Game On! The one they're going to play today for the grand opening."

The other goddessgirls, including her BFFs,

looked at her in surprise. Pheme had seemed ready to push for more on Hades' and Persephone's secret project. However, now she fixed her gaze on Artemis. "Ooh. Tell me more."

Pandora nodded. "Yeah, like how can I win?"

The others laughed. Artemis adjusted the quiver of arrows that hung over her shoulder and shook her head. "Can't tell you anything more. All details are top secret."

"C'mon," Pheme wheedled. "Just a teeny-weeny clue hinting at what the game's about? I'll die if you don't tell me."

"You're an immortal. You can't die," teased Artemis. "Besides, you'll see for yourself when the game opens an hour from now."

"But—" Pheme continued, looking determined.

Artemis held up a hand. "Okay, okay. I'll give

you one clue: Today's game might turn out to be a bit *bor*ing."

"Oh no, really?" said Athena, frowning a little. "Heracles will be so disappointed."

Clotho recalled reading in Pheme's column that that superstrong mortal boy had become her crush after she helped him complete a series of tasks called labors. Mortals weren't the only ones fascinated with the lives of immortals. The Fates kept up with news of them too!

Artemis grinned big at Athena. "Don't worry, you'll both still love the game, promise."

Pandora drew her head back in confusion. "Even though it's boring? How can that be?" Seemed this girl couldn't say anything unless it was in the form of a question.

Artemis pinched the tips of her thumb and index

finger together and drew them across her mouth. "My lips are sealed. Come to the grand opening if you want to know more."

If only I could! thought Clotho. But that was impossible. She'd already broken Zeus's rule enough for one day. She edged closer to the door again. It was past time to get going. She had only been at the IM for half an hour and already had spoken to *two* mortals. That was two more than Zeus or her sisters would consider okay!

"Oh, look how cute!" Aphrodite said suddenly. On her way out, Clotho glanced over her shoulder to see her and Persephone standing by the animal cookie display.

"I love this little knitted cat finger puppet!" Persephone enthused. She stuck it on her index finger. "Meow. Meow. I'd like some milk, please," she made the cat say.

The other girls gathered around, oohing and aahing at the puppets and trying them on their fingers too. "Who made these?" "Is there a pattern to make more?" "Are they for sale?" the girls wanted to know.

Cassandra looked baffled. "I don't know where they came from. They are cute, though. *Really* cute."

A warm, happy feeling spread through Clotho. It was a thrill to hear these girls compliment her creative knitting projects.

When a group of mortal customers entered the store, she quickly stuffed her papyrus sack of treats into her travel bag, then swung the bag over her shoulder and slipped out the door.

4

Arachne's Sewing Supplies

ONCE OUTSIDE THE BAKERY, CLOTHO TOOK off walking toward the Immortal Marketplace exit. But her feet faltered as a thought came to her. Maybe she could just take a quick look at that shop Hermes had mentioned as long as she was here. If she kept to herself from now on, speaking to no one, she wouldn't be breaking Zeus's no-mingling-with-mortals rule again.

She might as well get the wool and yarn she needed, right? That would be easier than finding sheep to shear. Plus, she could probably find ready-made green yarn at the shop, so she wouldn't have to do any dyeing in order to knit a serpent family. A win-win!

Besides, hadn't her sisters been coming to the IM to pick up mail from Hermes every week since forever? Without telling her? Checking out wool and knitting supplies seemed to her to be every bit as good a reason to explore the IM as picking up mail. Better, really. Because who needed to read that mean ol' mortal mail?

"Lachesis and Atropos shouldn't always get to tell me what to do," she murmured to herself. "I only need to do better at obeying *Zeus's* rules."

Fired up by that notion, she reversed direction. Now she walked at a brisk pace, her head turning back and forth as she searched for the sewing shop. Along the way, she took the papyrus bakery sack from her travel bag and pulled out the Oracle-O fortune cookie. When she crunched into it, the cookie announced: "Oh, what a tangled web you'll weave, when first you practice to deceive."

She scrunched her nose quizzically. "Huh? Are you sure you're not mislabeled, cookie? I think you must be an Opposite Oracle-O. Because I'm not dishonest." Then an uncomfortable thought struck her. "Oh, wait, maybe I have been just a teensy bit dishonest today. Because I've been talking to mortals here at the IM. Is that what you mean?" she murmured to the cookie. No reply. She sighed. "Well, thank you for the fortune anyway. You are delicious. And *that's* no lie!"

Crunch! She finished the cookie off in three bites, then stashed the bakery sack back in her travel bag again and pushed her guilty feelings about being here to the back of her mind. The stores she was passing were so intriguing. She saw a shop called Mighty Fighty that had a window display of armor and weapons. And a wedding shop full of fancy dresses and gifts called Hera's Happy Endings. Over the years she and her sisters had learned a lot about immortals. For instance, Hera was Zeus's wife and Athena's stepmom.

There was also Demeter's Daisies, Daffodils, and Floral Delights. Demeter was Persephone's mom, she recalled. The shop's bright green doors were propped open by various potted plants. Clotho paused to sniff a bunch of yellow flowers for sale. When she got too close to one of the flowers, it snapped at her nose!

Finally she spotted a glass-fronted store called

Arachne's Sewing Supplies across an atrium. She hurried over to it. A sign in its window read: GONE OUT OF BUSINESS.

Unfortunately, paper shades covered the inside of the shop's large glass door and all its windows. She couldn't see in to find out if it still contained any wool or yarn now that it was permanently closed. She tried turning the doorknob. *Drat.* It was locked.

Cupping her hands around her eyes, she attempted to peer in through a narrow gap between one of the shades and the edge of the shop door. She leaned close, her nose pushing against the glass.

Creak! She stumbled forward a few steps. To her surprise, her weight had pushed the door inward a few inches. It turned out that although the knob was locked, the door hadn't been pulled all the way closed, and so it wasn't latched. *Score!*

She decided to sneak in and take a look around, get what she needed, and then sneak out. No problem, right? Hermes had said it was okay to take supplies, so . . .

Clotho checked over her shoulder to be sure no one in the IM atrium was watching her. Even if it was okay to go inside, she didn't want anyone to see and start asking questions. As she was glancing around, she caught the eye of a mortal boy one store over. He had spiky hair and wore a green cape—and he was rushing in her direction! Startled, she drew back, but then he angled sharply to run across the atrium.

Her eyes followed him as he went over to stand at the end of a long line of kids queuing up outside another shop's huge arched entrance. Big, blinking, candlelit letters across the front of that shop proclaimed its name to be Game On! The new place everyone was so excited about. A banner above the sign read: GRAND-OPENING EVENT TODAY!

Everyone in line was focused on the new shop. Neither the caped boy nor anyone else appeared to be paying her the least bit of attention. Quickly Clotho pushed the door of the sewing shop farther open and slipped inside.

Phew. Made it! She leaned back against the door. It closed and latched behind her with a *snick*. When she gazed around the shop interior, she gasped. Because . . . *woo-hoo*! This place was a crafter's paradise! Despite having gone out of business, it was still well stocked with fabric, yarn, and all kinds of supplies.

Since no one outside the shop could see in through the shades covering the glass door and windows, she decided to take her time investigating. Spotting some stairs at the back of the shop, she headed there first and set her heavy travel bag down on the bottom step. She wiggled her shoulders up and down, back and forth. They kind of hurt from carrying all her junk around with her all the time.

The store looked a bit gloomy. And it had a slightly musty smell, like it had been abandoned for quite a while. Tall bolts of fabric stood on end on long rows of shelves. They were tilted at an angle, as if they'd gotten tired of standing upright with no customers in sight and had given in to slumping over. The floor was covered with a thin layer of dust.

Still, as Clotho wandered around, her excitement grew. Everywhere she looked, she saw stuff she and her sisters could use: yarn, thread, scissors, pins, embroidery hoops, small silver needles for sewing, brightly colored long needles for knitting, and hooks for crocheting.

Much like the Oracle-O Bakery, everything here was well organized. She admired one entire wall lined with shelves and cubbies that were stuffed with skeins and balls of yarn of any color she could ever want. Upon closer inspection, however, she noticed that many of the yarn skeins were droopy and the balls flattened. She pulled a bright blue ball from a cubby. This caused a small puff of dust to kick up and made her sneeze. *Achoo!*

Noticing a large loom for weaving cloth that had been set up in one corner of the shop, she went over to check it out. The loom wasn't threaded. If Lachesis were here she'd thread the thing up in a hot minute! That girl loved to weave and wouldn't have been able to resist. And all those scissors hanging on a turquoise pegboard? Clotho didn't know why you would need so many differently shaped blades, but Atropos would know the special use for each one. She'd go crazy over them.

Then Clotho spotted her own little piece of crafty heaven in the center of the shop. Bins and bins that held everything from alpaca fleece to angora wool to sheep's wool to cotton and silk. *Wowza!*

She rushed over to her bag and grabbed her distaff and spindle. Then she returned to dust off a stool near the bins and sit. In a flash she became absorbed in spinning the sheep and angora wool to test their textures. Spinning required multitasking. It wasn't easy to control the amount of fiber you were twisting while spinning it. It was sort of like trying to pat your head and rub your tummy at the same time!

Lulled as she was by the familiar and comfortable

task, a couple of hours passed without Clotho realizing it. At last she stood and reached her arms high in a stretch. After lowering them, she turned in a circle to again gaze upon the riches surrounding her. To think that no one was using any of this. What a waste.

An idea took shape in her brain. Why not come here every day to spin, knit, and crochet stuff? Her sisters wouldn't have to know. It wasn't exactly lying to leave out information, was it?

And next visit, she wouldn't talk to any mortals. None. Zip. She could still peek out at them and pretend to herself that she was friends with some of them without them knowing. No rule against that. Doing so would make her feel less, well . . . less lonely. Sure, she knew her sisters cared about her, but it had been fun to be around other girls besides them today.

Quickly Clotho pulled some raw sheep's wool from one of the bins. She would take it with her to the constellation tonight and spin it. Then tomorrow morning, she'd return here and knit some green yarn into serpent puppets. Even though Hermes had said it was okay to take what she needed, she decided to leave some drachmas on a dusty counter in payment for what she was taking. If someone did indeed still own the shop and happened by at some point, they'd no doubt appreciate the money she left.

"Mew. Mew."

Wait—what was that? The sound was coming from over by the stairs. From a kitten! It was now perched on the bottom step, sniffing around her bag.

Moving toward the kitten, she extended her hand in a friendly way, cooing in a sweet voice. "Hello, kitty. Where'd you come from?" When she got close enough, she stroked the top of its head with her fingertips.

It cocked its fuzzy head cutely, gazing at her with big green eyes. Then it rolled over in a long stretch. It even let her pick it up. She dropped down to sit on the bottom step, then set the kitten in her lap and ran a hand lightly over its soft white fur. Snuggling in, it began to purr in a soft rumble she could feel under her palm. Her heart melted like chocolate in the sun.

"Aww! You are *sooo* adorable. But what are you doing all alone? How'd you get in here?"

"Purrr," the kitten replied.

"Sorry, I don't actually speak cat language." She could feel its ribs, she realized. "You hungry?" She pulled the bakery sack from her travel bag, then shared some crumbled cookie tidbits. Although it probably wasn't the healthiest cat food ever, the kitten ate greedily.

Hearing a dripping sound coming from somewhere, Clotho went to investigate, leaving the kitten to eat. Behind the stairs she found a small kitchenette with a sink and cupboards, a little table, four chairs, and some dishes. She got a bowl and filled it with water.

While carrying it back, she spotted a kitten-size hole along one wall near the floor. It led directly from the IM to outdoors. Mystery solved—that had to be how the kitten had gotten in here. By the time she reached the stairs again, the kitten had finished the snack crumbles. Thirstily it drank the water she offered, then licked its fur for a while.

Clotho tried playing with the cutie-pie fur ball, dragging a piece of yarn across the floor for it to chase.

It attacked. It pounced. Sooo adorbs! Watching it, she felt a tug at her heart. She'd never told her sisters she yearned for a pet. What if she took this one with her when she left here? Maybe she could carry it around in her bag? No, that wouldn't be responsible. This kitten had made a home for itself in here. It wouldn't be fair to make it homeless like she was.

Eventually the kitten got tired and curled up in a basket of unspun wool for a nap. Clotho petted it and petted it, falling completely in love. It purred loudly for her, almost seeming to smile.

This kitten needed her. Not just for food and water, but also for *love*. It was probably every bit as lonely as that serpent back in Colchis. Remembering her plan to return to the shop every day, she figured she now had an even more important reason to do so. She needed to care for this kitten! She'd feed it, play with it, and love it, and it would love her back, she thought with a happy sigh.

Suddenly a new thought struck her. "I guess you don't already belong to anyone, huh, little kitten?"

"It's a stray," a teeny, squeaky voice informed her. "Wanders in here to keep me company and sleeps inside the shop sometimes."

Clotho jumped up and her head whipped around. Her eyes swept the room, looking for the owner of the voice. "Huh? Who said that?"

"Me," squeaked the voice.

It was coming from upstairs, Clotho realized. She went to investigate and was halfway up the steps when she passed through some almost-invisible sticky strands, which clung to her. "Ew! Yuck. Spiderwebs." She batted them away.

"Hey, watch it! Took me ten minutes to spin that

web," grumped that same teeny, squeaky voice.

Clotho froze. "Who said that?"

"Me. The owner of this store, who'd you think?"

"Owner?" Her heart sank, her dream of making this into her own personal daytime workspace and hangout dimming like a dying candle. She squinted into the semidarkness at the top of the stairs, where the voice was coming from. "Sorry, I didn't mean to trespass or anything. Hermes told me about this shop and I just *had* to see it. The door wasn't closed all the way, so I was hoping to take some wool. I left some drachmas on the counter to pay for it. Um, who . . . where are you, anyway?"

She heard a small sigh. Then the voice came again. "Not everyone travels on big feet stomping across the ground like you, you know. I'm up here, foolish girl."

Clotho's gaze rose to another web, which hung high in a corner of the staircase where two walls met the ceiling. A brown spider sat upon it. And it was staring right at her with all eight of its beady, round eyes! Good thing she wasn't afraid of spiders. In fact she actually found them interesting. She stepped closer.

That was when she noticed the single word woven into the web: ARACHNE.

"Are you . . . Arachne?" Clotho guessed, staring up at the creature.

The spider puffed herself up, appearing pleased. "Why, yes. I'm not surprised you've heard of me. I was once pretty famous."

"Well, your name *is* on the sign outside the shop. And in your web up there too, so it wasn't hard to guess." Clotho tilted her head, a little confused. "I've

never met a talking spider, though. Or heard of a spider owning a store, either. I didn't think bugs were able to do stuff like that."

"Bug? No way. I'm an arachnid!" huffed Arachne.

But Clotho wasn't really listening. Because she'd just noticed there were other spiderwebs along the ceiling with shocking words woven into them, such as THEENY IS A MEANIE! ZEUS IS A GOOSE! It was a well-known fact that Theeny was Zeus's nickname for his beloved daughter Athena.

Clotho pointed at the web words in horror. "Did you spin those sayings? They could get you in a lot of trouble."

"Trouble, schmubble," muttered Arachne. Letting out a single long, silvery thread, she lowered herself to hang about a foot above Clotho's nose. "I'm no stranger to trouble. Do you think I've always been

a spider? Nope! I was once a mortal. A magnificent weaver, the best on Earth, and this was my shop. Until that goddessgirl Athena ruined things by turning me into an arachnid. I had to crawl all the way back here after losing a weaving contest to her. I've never forgiven her."

"Athena invented weaving, right?" Clotho mused aloud. "So I'm wondering why she would turn a great weaver like you into a spider."

A shifty look came into Arachne's eyeballs. She raised one hairy leg, then lowered it. Probably a spider's version of a shrug. "No clue. Well, I may have woven a tapestry of Zeus dancing around with a thunderbolt stuck in his foot and his tunic on fire. Hilarious, right? Some immortals can't take a joke."

Clotho gasped. "What? That's terrible. No wonder you got in trouble!"

The spider slid down a few more inches of silver thread to dangle closer. "Yeah, well, I still don't think it was fair. So what's your name, anyway?" Arachne asked her, changing the subject.

"Clotho," said Clotho. Then she winced. She'd done it again! Her and her big mouth. But this spider likely had no more idea of who she was than the girls in the bakery had. "Anyway, I guess I should get going." She turned to leave.

"Wait! Don't you want to see the rest of my shop? C'mon." Arachne sped up her sticky vertical thread and took off across the ceiling, moving farther upstairs. "Besides my room, there are three more little rooms up here. Plus a bathroom."

Clotho considered this information as she climbed the rest of the way up the stairs and peeked inside each room. Her heart began to pound with excitement. It was just the way she'd always imagined her home might be. Three rooms, one for her and for each of her sisters, where they could keep their stuff and be private when they wanted to. And downstairs, some hangout space and a kitchen. Plus, a big, fat bonus—the shop. This place had all the space and supplies they could ever need!

It was perfect except for two things. First, Arachne owned all of this. And second, Clotho's sisters didn't seem to want a permanent home. Still, she could so easily picture them all working here at night on the Destiny List. Most IM shops would close once it grew dark, so no mortals would be around then. *If only*.

Just then the sounds of distant footsteps, cheers, and laughter floated up to her ears. Had someone else entered the shop? Clotho crept back downstairs but saw no one. The sounds were coming from out in the atrium. She went over to the door, lifted the edge of the shade covering it, and peeked out. Across the atrium, the long line of people had finally begun moving into Game On!

She glanced back at the kitten and saw that it was still sleeping atop the basket of wool. Cassandra had said there would be food at that grand-opening event across the way. Including little sandwiches. Possibly she could find something there like tuna fish that would be more appropriate to feed a kitten. She ran over and grabbed her bag.

"Arachne? I'm going to that new gaming shop to see if there are any snacks the kitten might like. Be right back," she called in the direction of the stairs. No answer from the spider. "I'll be back!" Clotho called again, louder this time. Still no answer.

Shrugging, she slung the straps of her travel

bag over one shoulder. After pinching off a piece of sheep's wool from a bundle in one of the baskets, she stepped outside the shop. Before the door could click tight behind her, she carefully slipped the hunk of wool between the lock mechanism and its counterpart in the door frame. Then she gently closed it. There was no click sound. Satisfied that the door would appear to passersby to be securely latched (even though it wasn't), she hurried across the atrium to join the throng heading into the brand-new Game On!

5

Game On!

AFTER FIFTEEN MINUTES SPENT IN LINE, Clotho was finally moving through the tall arched entrance to Game On! The arch was carved with fancy scrollwork that was entwined with figures of the goddesses and gods of Mount Olympus fighting against the Titans in a famous war called the Titanomachy. There was Zeus hurling a mighty thunderbolt. And Athena holding an owl that represented her famed wisdom. And Ares, the god of war, holding a spear high as if poised to strike down enemies.

Once beyond the arch, Clotho found herself in a lobby with several booths displaying game-related merchandise for sale. She kept going. A mortal employee dressed in an oracle costume and wearing a sparkly Game On! hat came over to her. "Welcome! I predict you will have fun at Game On!" he said. Then he pulled a thumb-size stone with a number painted on it from a bag he carried. "For choosing team captains today," he informed her.

Huh? Since she wasn't supposed to talk to mortals, Clotho silently pocketed the stone. She only smiled as he pinned a button to her chiton that read GAME ON! and waved her through another arch.

Once past the second arch she wound up standing in a dimly lit, enormous room packed with eager young mortal and immortal customers who'd come for the grand opening. She scanned the crowd and spotted Aphrodite, Athena, and Pandora. Cassandra had likely stayed behind in the bakery, hoping to sell goodies to customers who wandered by, as well as to help prepare for Zeus's birthday party tomorrow.

Some godboys were standing near the MOA goddessgirls. She easily recognized Ares who held his spear and wore a helmet. And Poseidon, the god of the sea, who was holding a drippy three-pronged trident. And was that black-haired godboy with him Apollo? Probably. He looked a lot like Artemis, his twin. However, Artemis was nowhere to be seen. Neither was Persephone.

Squinting, Clotho noticed an enormous, deep pit in the center of the room and, at the room's far end, a small stage. At one side of the stage was a long, fancy table laden with snacks and drinks, likely all supplied by Cassandra's bakery. And maybe including (fingers crossed) something a kitten would like! Lots of kids were gathering around the table, putting goodies on small plates and then wandering off to munch them. She started sidling her way toward the table to check out the offerings, but halted in her tracks when trumpets blared, grabbing everyone's attention.

A spotlight flashed onto a man and woman wearing golden crowns, who came to stand atop the small stage. The man lifted his arms and spoke in a voice that commanded everyone's attention. "Greetings, one and all! I am King Oeneus, ruler of Calydon on mainland Greece, east of the Ionian Sea."

The woman beside him smiled brightly and added, "And I am Queen Althea of Calydon. We humbly welcome you, immortals, mortals, and beasts, to the grand opening of our new shop, Game On!" The pair whipped their purple velvet capes in grand flourishes and bowed low. Thunderous whoops and cheers sounded from the excited crowd.

Beasts? thought Clotho. Her eyes darted around, finally spotting two centaurs standing over in a corner. They had the upper bodies of humans and the lower bodies and legs of horses. The reddish-brown hair on their heads matched that on their haunches.

After the royals straightened, the king continued speaking in a loud voice while waving his arms excitedly, sort of like an energetic music conductor or a magician. "Today we open with our first game. Prepare to witness a sensational spectacle! Behold . . . *the arena*!"

At his words, the hundreds of candles in the chandeliers that hung from the ceiling of the large room suddenly brightened. What had at first appeared to be a mysterious dark pit was now revealed to be a round sunken arena that took up most of the floor space in the center of the room.

Everyone, including Clotho, rushed to stand along a waist-high railing to look down into the arena some twenty feet below. At the moment, it was empty of people. Two rows of bleacher seats ringed its upper edge just below the railing, but no one took a seat just yet.

Behind them on the little stage, the king chose that moment to announce, "Today, two teams will battle it out in that arena in a test of skill the likes of which has never been seen before!"

A thrilled gasp rippled over the crowd, and excited chatter broke out. "This is gonna be the coolest thing ever!" "Oh my gods!" "Can*not* wait!"

Since all attention was focused on the arena in anticipation of what might happen there soon, Clotho *could* have headed for the snack table. *Should* have, and then gotten herself outta there.

But like the others, she was irresistibly drawn to examine the arena. It was similar to the one at the Colosseum in Rome, Italy, she couldn't help noticing. She and her sisters sometimes met there to spin mortal fates. However, the Roman Colosseum was outdoors and much bigger, whereas Game On! had a domed ceiling to keep weather out.

Thinking of the bakery she'd visited earlier, she decided that this arena's setup was sort of like a gigantic doughnut—the doughy part being the balcony where she and everyone else now stood, and the doughnut hole being the actual arena in the middle, sunken more than one floor below. It was divided into thirds, sort of like three pizza slices. Only, one of the pizza slices was currently lit for a game, while the other two were curtained off.

Clotho leaned forward and craned her neck to study the one-third part of the arena where the upcoming game was apparently to be played. *Wowza!* It was amazing! An elaborate set that included sculpted hills, towers, and randomly placed obstacles like craggy rock towers and trees. There were rope ladders, trampolines, and a waterfall, too. The walls surrounding the arena were painted with figures resembling famous Greek statues and landmarks in scenes that celebrated glorious feats of the goddesses and gods.

"It's mega-awesome!" a strong-looking mortal boy shouted out from beside her. "But who gets to be on the teams?" The boy was holding a very large

club as if it weighed nothing at all. This must be Heracles! He was one of the few exceptional mortals who attended Mount Olympus Academy. Just beyond him at the railing stood Ares, Aphrodite, and Athena.

King Oeneus spoke again, confirming her guess about the boy's identity. "Glad you asked, Heracles! It is now time to choose our two captains, who will then get a chance to select their team members. You should all have received a numbered stone upon entering Game On! My queen will randomly choose the first team captain by calling out a number. Please check it against your stone."

A hush fell. The queen reached into a bag and pulled from it a small piece of papyrus. After reading something written upon it, she called out, "Number fifty-one!"

There were murmurs, and then a mortal boy's voice rose from the crowd. "Hey! That's my number, Mom!"

"Looks like Prince Meleager will be the first team captain," said the happily surprised queen. She clasped her hands in delight and smiled at her son with great affection as he showed off for everyone, making muscle poses.

Clotho cocked her head to study the prince. *Meleager?* Why did that name sound so familiar? And why did hearing it make her feel so . . . *uneasy*? Like with all mortals, she had surely read his name from the Destiny List on the day he was born. But there had been so many names over the years, she couldn't remember them all. For example, she hadn't recalled Cassandra's or Pandora's names when she'd met them today. So what was different about Meleager that made her recall his?

"Today's other team captain will be . . ." The king pulled another piece of papyrus from the bag. After glancing at it, he paused to draw out the tension, then loudly called out, "Number twenty-five!"

At his words, a tall, slender young mortal woman with hair as long and golden as Aphrodite's sprang from the crowd to more cheers. She wore a white chiton and matching sandals, and had the muscular legs of a runner. "That's me! I'm Atalanta!" she announced, holding up a stone painted with the matching number.

"Congratulations, captains! You may now each select four additional players from among those assembled here to be on your teams. No Mount Olympus Academy students for this first game, though, in order to keep skills fairly evenly matched," directed the queen. Disappointed grumbles came from some of the MOA-ers. "Don't worry," the queen told them, "you'll be able to play a second version of this game tomorrow, with new additions to make the battle even more challenging. And another all-new game will be introduced tomorrow for you to test-run as well!" Her words soothed the MOA students, instantly changing their grumbles to cheers.

"Now, Meleager, since you drew the higher number, you may choose your team first," the king chimed in.

Everyone turned toward the prince, awaiting his teammate choices. But Meleager just stood there. He was staring at Atalanta, who was standing only a few feet away from him. The look on his face was weird, sort of lovey-dovey.

Observing this from a distance, Aphrodite

smiled. Clotho heard her murmur, "I smell an insta-crush."

"'Insta'?" echoed Athena. "Oh, I get it—short for 'instant,' as in liking someone at first sight?"

Ares' eyebrows rose as he interrupted to ask Aphrodite, "Who—you mean Meleager and Atalanta?"

Nodding, she replied, "Mm-hm. That boy is crushing on Atalanta or my title isn't goddessgirl of *love* and beauty."

When Meleager continued to stare at Atalanta without speaking, Atalanta planted her hands on her hips and frowned at him. "C'mon. Choose, dude! Let's get this show on the road!"

"Ha! Atalanta has got to be at least sixteen or seventeen years old," Ares scoffed quietly to Aphrodite. "Meleager's our age, like twelve or thirteen. No way she's going to see him as anything but a kid."

Aphrodite nodded. "Alas for Meleager, you're right. Although Atalanta is very young-looking, I happen to know that she's nineteen and got married recently, a romance I helped to blossom. Matters of the heart are often complicated." She exchanged a smile with Ares. His eyes on hers went goo-goo sweet for a moment. The two of them were crushes, Clotho had read somewhere. Probably in Pheme's gossip column.

Atalanta's urging seemed to temporarily shake Meleager out of his smitten daze. His gaze whipped across all the faces of those standing in the balcony as he prepared to select his team members.

Clotho decided she had lingered long enough. While everyone's attention was on Meleager, she edged away from the crowd at the railing, eyeing the snack table again.

As she sidled toward it, she heard the prince

announce, "I pick my cousins Plexippus and Toxeus. And the centaurs Hylaeus and Rhaecus." Cheers sounded, and Clotho glanced back to see two red-haired, freckle-faced guys move to stand at his side. One looked maybe fourteen years old and the other maybe fifteen. The pair of centaurs she'd noticed earlier clip-clopped over to him as well to round out his team.

Atalanta made her first choices in a sure voice. "I choose two of my fellow Argonauts—Jason and Euphemus. They've got skills!"

When the crowd chuckled at her enthusiasm, she set a hand at her hip. "What? They do! I ought to know. I sailed with them and the other Argonauts on the ship *Argo*. And guess who won the Golden Fleece?" She tapped a fingertip on her chin, pretending to think hard.

"The Argonauts!" the crowd whooped, supplying her with an answer she already knew. Jason and Euphemus raced over to join her, and the three of them punched victorious fists high. Clotho grinned. Those mortals had been instrumental in stealing the famed Golden Fleece from that oak tree the Fates had sat in last night!

"Next, I choose Theseus," Atalanta said. "To honor his bravery in defeating the very scary Minotaur, a monster at King Minos's amusement park on the island of Crete." More cheers sounded as her third choice, a boy with dreadlocks and brown eyes, shot over to join her.

Everyone held their breath as she surveyed the crowd, searching out a final team member. Many tried to catch her eye, including a mortal girl named Medusa, who had a dozen snakes for hair. Right now

they were all wiggling wildly and gesturing toward Medusa for consideration, even though she probably wasn't eligible due to being one of those special mortals who was a student at MOA.

Finally Clotho made it to the snack table. Her brown eyes went wide as they took in the bounty upon it. There was plenty here that a kitten might enjoy—little tuna sandwiches, chicken rolls, beef tips, and more. *Score!* She opened her bag, digging around for something to use as a food container.

"Watch out, will you? You trying to squash me or something?" complained a tiny, squeaky voice from within her bag.

Huh? Were her finger puppets talking now, or what? Clotho peered deeper inside her bag, then blinked. Eight little beady eyes stared back up at her. She jerked back in surprise, accidentally elbowing a

flask of water sitting on the edge of the table. *Crash!* The sound of the flask hitting the floor echoed into the quiet that had fallen over the crowd in the balcony as they awaited Atalanta's final choice.

"Calm down. It's just me," said the tiny voice.

"Arachne?" Clotho hissed. "How did you get here?"

"Hopped on your shoulder back in the shop stairwell, then parachuted via web strand into your bag when you picked it up. Easy-peasy," that annoying spider explained.

Just then, a shout rang out from Atalanta. "You! I choose you! What's your name?"

When no one responded, Clotho glanced around. *Oh no!* Atalanta was pointing. Right. At. *Her!*

Rising to her feet, Clotho grabbed her bag, slinging its straps over one shoulder again with the spider

inside. "Who, me? I'm, uh, I'm Clotho," she blurted out. *Argh!* Third time in a row she'd given her real name! Too late to make up a fake name now. But just as before no one seemed to realize she was one of the Fates, so she supposed it didn't really matter.

A path through the crowd opened between her and Atalanta. Smiling big, the young woman jogged over and clapped a friendly arm around her. "Perfect-o! Clotho is a cool-o name-o," she said, playfully mimicking the *o* sound at the end of Clotho's name. "Welcome to Team Atalanta!"

Clotho tried to pull away. "No! You don't want me on your team-o. I mean team. I'm not really good at games. Or sports. I knit." Soft giggles rippled through the balcony at her goofy reply.

Atalanta just looked at her curiously as if she wasn't sure whether to believe her or not. Then

she grinned and elbowed her. "Ha-ha! Good one. S'okay. I like to pick a wild card in team sports. Keeps things interesting. Besides, smarts are mostly what's needed in any competition, and you look smart to me. You'll do fine."

Clotho shook her head in protest. "I'm honored to be chosen, but—" Before she could politely but firmly decline, Atalanta tugged her back through the crowd. (That girl was strong!) Within seconds they'd joined the eight others standing near the king and queen's stage.

"Let's hear it for Team Meleager and Team Atalanta! Good luck to both," declared Oeneus and Althea.

Clotho gazed around. The audience of immortals and mortals was now wildly cheering. Though she'd only read three of those letters that unhappy mortals had sent to her and her sisters, she was certain she'd never forget a single hurtful word of what they'd said. So it felt kind of good to hear everyone, especially the mortals here, rooting for her.

Before she knew it, two grinning stagehands wearing sparkly Game On! hats were herding all ten participants down a ramp, heading for the arena below. As they walked, Clotho and the others waved and smiled at the cheering onlookers, who watched their progress from up on the balcony.

What would happen if she performed well in these games? Clotho wondered dreamily. If mortals somehow learned she was a Fate, brave deeds done by her in the upcoming challenge might make them think better of her and her sisters.

Clank! The sound of the arena's metal gate swinging shut behind her and the other team members

pulled her out of her wistful daydreaming. Her footsteps slowed. Wait a minute. What was she thinking? That fantasy could never be. Zeus and her two sisters were totally against the Fates ever revealing their identities to mortals or hanging out with them. She needed to get out of here, pronto.

Whirling around, she saw that she was trapped in the arena! Dazzled by mortal cheers, she'd been lulled into making a very big mistake. Competing in this game was definitely going to result in her mingling with mortals. Which would break Zeus's third rule for what felt like the bazillionth time today!

She ran back to send a pleading look through the bars of the metal gate at the two stagehands who'd remained on the ramp beyond it. "Wait! Yoo-hoo! Let me out. I—I can't play after all," she told them.

One of them peered closely at her through the bars. "You sick?"

"Well, no," Clotho admitted.

"Then you stay. And you play," ordered the other stagehand. "Once this gate is closed, it won't reopen till the winning team is declared. Off with you! Go suit up in your combat gear with your team."

"Wait—" Clotho started to argue, but the stagehands were already tromping away.

Bawk! Bawk! Arachne's voice floated up to her from inside her travel bag. That spider was making chicken noises at her?

"Hush! I am not a scaredy-cat—er, chicken," Clotho hissed at Arachne. "I simply cannot be here. Zeus wouldn't like it."

Before Arachne could reply, Atalanta clapped a hand on Clotho's shoulder. Clotho sagged a little.

Because . . . *Ow!* Her team captain did not know her own strength!

"C'mon, Clotho!" Atalanta urged. "This is gonna be so-o fun-o!" She giggled. Apparently, she really, really thought it was funny to mimic Clotho's name by adding *o*s to the ends of other words. Her grin was so friendly, though, that it was kind of flattering. This was how friends probably treated one another, she decided, bestowing cute nicknames. Was Atalanta trying to be her friend?

She let Atalanta lead her away from the gate and over to the cubbies along one wall of the arena. There, like everyone else, Clotho stowed her bag and sandals, then dressed in combat gear, including a helmet, boots, and a shield. Then the others picked out spears and arrows. *Gulp!* Clotho didn't know how to use either!

"Ya know, being the only female crew member sailing the *Argo* got really old," Atalanta said to her as they suited up. "Nice to have you aboard for this game. I figure us women-os gotta stick together, righty-o? Show the boy-os our girl power!"

Clotho smiled weakly. "Yeah. Um, stick together . . . girl power . . . righty-o." Having no other choice, once they'd all been properly outfitted, she followed Atalanta and other players into the arena.

Their footsteps seemed to activate some kind of magic. Instantly, everything in the arena—landscape features and obstacles alike—began to come alive and shift position and even change shape! Trees swayed. Hills sprouted flowers or brambles, which formed hedges, which then turned into animal topiaries. Towers and rocks grew smaller, then larger, smoother, then craggier, and then reverted back again. Large and small trampolines bounced themselves around the arena aimlessly, dipping low as if inviting players to jump up and down on them.

Atalanta clapped her hands, and her eyes sparkled. "Ooh! It's like an enchanted obstacle course!"

"Yeah!" Clotho grinned because Atalanta's excitement was kind of catching. "Maybe this game will turn out to be sort of fun after all."

"Fun, yes!" the king announced from the balcony, overhearing her. "However, only one team will survive."

"S-s-survive?" snorted one of the centaurs. He sounded as nervous as Clotho suddenly felt. What had she gotten herself into?

6

Ready, Set, Attack!

"FEAR NOT. IT'S ALL IN FUN," QUEEN ALTHEA TOLD everyone with a bright, reassuring smile. "The spears and arrows used in our game cannot cause injury."

By now she and King Oeneus had come to sit grandly in one of the rows of seats that ringed the balcony overlooking the brightly lit third of the arena where the game would commence. Others in the audience either sat in the seats as well or stood along the railing as they prepared to watch the contest unfold.

"The queen speaks true, team members!" the king called out to the arena. "All weapons in Game On! are made of magic. Your spears and arrows appear dangerous but won't do any real harm. Each time you are struck with one from an opposing team member, a temporary red *X* will magically appear on your skin. Three *X*s mean you're out, out, out of the competition! The team with the most players still standing in the arena when you hear the sound of a lute wins the game!"

There was a brief pause as the queen handed the king a scroll; then he went on. "Before we begin the very first game ever to be played in this stupendous arena, I would like to take a moment to solemnly dedicate our new shop in honor of the goddesses

and gods of Mount Olympus." He ceremoniously whipped open the scroll and began reciting from an alphabetical list of all the honored immortals. "Amphitrite, Antheia, Aphrodite, Apollo, Ares, Athena . . ."

Whoa! Until now, Clotho had never realized how many immortals' names started with the letter *A*! The scroll the king was reading from was a long one. So to pass the time, she, her four teammates, and the five members of the other team did stretches. She was doing jumping jacks when an all-too-familiar teeny voice piped up from somewhere below her left ear.

"That king is just trying to pump up the egos of those goddesses and gods. As if they weren't already stuck-up enough," the voice complained.

Huh? Good thing she didn't have arachnophobia

(which was a fancy name for fear of spiders). Because when Clotho glanced sideways, she saw that Arachne was perched on her left shoulder! Sometime earlier, without her noticing, that wacky spider had managed to crawl out of her travel bag and up her arm. And, as usual, Arachne was back to insulting immortals. Clotho tried not to take offense, even though she was immortal too. She needed to stay on this spider's good side if she wanted permission to work in her shop.

"You shouldn't be here," she warned the spider. "What if you fall off and get stomped on? This arena is way too dangerous for someone so small."

"Don't worry," said Arachne. "My sticky feet can hang on to anything. And me being here is a win-win situation for the two of us. I get out of the shop to have some fun for a change. And you get my help.

With my eight eyes to watch out for you, you could actually win this game."

"Hey, Clotho, stop giving yourself a pep talk and get over here, girl," Atalanta called just then. Because Arachne was too tiny for her to notice, she'd obviously thought Clotho had been speaking to herself!

Clotho looked over and saw that, as the king droned on, some team members had begun trying out the equipment in the arena. Atalanta was currently boinging around on the arena floor, which seemed to be every bit as bouncy as the mobile trampolines.

"Watch!" Atalanta crouched low, then boinged up from the floor to land on a passing square trampoline. From there she proceeded to bounce high and do flips in the air.

When the moving trampoline veered close to Clotho, Atalanta grabbed on to her hand, pulling her up too. Surprised by this maneuver, Arachne let out a screech.

Atalanta winced at the ear-piercing sound. "Whoa! That's quite a screech you got there, Clotho."

Clotho didn't take time to explain that the screech had in fact come from a spider. Because she and Atalanta were suddenly having fun! They were boinging around, slapping hands, bumping elbows, and doing dance moves in midair, giggling all the while. When a star-shaped trampoline happened by, Clotho grabbed Atalanta's hand and they leaped from the square one over to it. After that, whenever a new trampoline bounced near, they'd switch again.

"Woo-hoo! Higher!" Arachne hollered. Her sticky spider feet really were having no trouble hanging on. After her initial surprise she was apparently having a blast.

"Yeah, higher! This is funtastic-o!" Atalanta said, mistakenly assuming that Clotho had been the one who'd done the woo-hooing.

Clotho did a backflip and grinned big at the athletic young woman. "Yeah, tons o' fun!" She'd never tried doing flips in the air while flying in her sandals. She'd been missing out!

In good spirits, the two of them began showing off, bouncing higher and higher, and doing even more daring flips and girl-power poses as they sprang from the trampolines. And with each bounce, they seemed to be gaining the favor of the crowd overlooking the arena. Enjoying their antics, the onlookers laughed and shouted encouragement. *Super!* thought Clotho. If the crowd liked them, they would probably root for their team once the games began. Though Clotho was having the best time ever, deep inside she was aware she was breaking the "no mingling" rule. She pushed away the thought. She'd never had a chance to hang out with anyone besides her sisters before, and this experience was amazing!

Eventually the king's words came to a halt as he ended his alphabetical list of honored immortals with ". . . and last but not least, Zeus." Probably relieved that the king was finally done, the audience clapped extra loud and called out hoorays. Down in the arena, the ten team members hopped off the trampolines and gathered to stare up at the king. All looked as curious as Clotho felt regarding how this game would begin.

King Oeneus had opened his mouth as if preparing to explain, when a voice blasted out from somewhere on the balcony. "What about my sister, Artemis? Why wasn't she on your list?" It was the godboy Apollo. And he was pointing an accusing finger at the king. The king froze, seemingly unable to come up with a reply.

Standing on the arena floor, Clotho heard Toxeus say to Meleager, "Good question. Did your dad leave Artemis out on purpose or what?"

Meleager shrugged uncertainly. "Dunno. But I do know immortals aren't going to be happy about this."

"Especially not Artemis," Atalanta put in.

They spoke freely in front of Clotho, not realizing that she, too, was an immortal. She lifted her eyes and scanned the crowd above them but didn't see the goddessgirl in question. "Where is Artemis, anyway?" she said to Atalanta. "I heard her talking about the game earlier this morning, and she sounded excited about it. In fact, she helped design it. So why isn't she here?"

Before Atalanta could respond, Ares stepped forward in the balcony to clap an arm on Apollo's shoulder. "Apollo's right. His sister has been dissed!"

7

Snort

COMPLAINTS AMONG THE IMMORTALS IN THE audience began to grow. It was an insult to all of them (Clotho, too) that one of their number had not been properly recognized. Poseidon thumped the handle end of his trident on the floor in annoyance. This caused a stream of water to shoot from the tops of its three sharp prongs, spraying those who stood nearby.

The murmurs got louder. "Artemis has been insulted by a mortal king!" "We immortals shouldn't put up with it." "She must be avenged!"

Mortals in the audience—as well as down in the arena—frowned, becoming restless and worried.

"Revenge first, questions later. Typical," remarked the teeny, squeaky voice of Arachne. The spider had to be thinking of how Athena had taken revenge on her after that weaving contest. Nevertheless, Clotho shushed her.

Overhearing, Atalanta quirked an eyebrow at Clotho, obviously mistaking Arachne's words for hers again. "Oh, I didn't mean—" Clotho started to say. But she fell silent when a girl's voice suddenly rang out.

"How dare you insult me!" It was Artemis at last! Every head whipped her way as she appeared on

the balcony to stand on the bleachers beside her brother. She gestured accusingly at the king with one hand, while keeping the other firmly behind her back. *Strange*, thought Clotho. Was the girl hiding something? "I cannot believe you left my name out of your list of honorees! Especially when I think of all the work I've done to help create this game. You have much to answer for!"

Yikes, thought Clotho. Artemis sounded super angry!

Apollo punched a fist high in the air. "You tell him, sis! You are a *goddess*. No mortal should ever disrespect you like that. Not even royalty!"

Clotho happened to look at the queen right then. To her surprise, she saw Althea wink at Artemis, who grinned back. *Huh? What was that all about?* It didn't make sense. Had she been mistaken about

the wink? Maybe the queen had gotten something in her eye and had been trying to blink it out. But that wouldn't explain the grin, and it really had looked like a wink.

As if truly frightened by Artemis's show of anger, the king got on his knees and clasped both hands to his chest. "Oh, Goddess, please forgive me," he wailed with melodramatic flair.

This was all kind of over-the-top, Clotho decided. And it didn't quite ring true. It was sort of like the king and Artemis were actors in a play, reciting lines they'd practiced many times over. What was going on here?

"Hmph. I will not forgive you so easily!" Artemis declared. The hand she'd been holding behind her back whipped forward. A papyrus scroll was clasped in her fist, and she unfurled it. "Good thing I just, uh, happen to have my MOA Revenge-ology class textscroll with me. I'll read aloud what it says right here in chapter six." She cleared her throat. "Ahem. 'Dealing with Disrespect: When a mortal insults a god or goddess, retribution is required.'" Having made her point, she let go of the end of the scroll. It rolled itself back up with a *snap*.

Weird coincidence that she just happened to have that scroll handy, thought Clotho. And that she had found the section within it about insulting an immortal so quickly.

Perched on a bleacher seat almost directly behind Artemis and Apollo, the gossipy Pheme was hastily scribbling on a notescroll she held. Everything that was happening here would no doubt show up in her *Teen Scrollazine* column this week.

"King Oeneus!" Artemis went on. "Your unfor-

givable slight to me cannot go unpunished. So, as befits my title as goddessgirl of the hunt, I will now unleash a true terror. One that will kick off your grand opening in a way no one will soon forget. After all, we wouldn't want things to get *bor*-ing!" Everyone gasped as she whipped out her bow and nocked an arrow. Surely she wouldn't send it flying toward the king, would she?

Grinning big, Artemis shot her arrow high. It burst a humungous bag that hung from the domed ceiling, unnoticed till now. Confetti rained from it down into the arena like sparkly, colorful snow. "I hereby command that the magical spears and arrows will go live in five, four, three, two, one!" she shouted. "Game On! Have fun, everyone!"

There was laughter, hooting, and cheering as Clotho and everyone else realized the great joke that

had just been played on them. The king's supposed insult had all been part of a plan. Artemis had merely *pretended* to be angry to make the opening of the game more dramatic! Apollo, Ares, and Poseidon looked as astonished as everyone else. Clotho guessed that Artemis hadn't even let her brother and his friends in on the surprise that she and the king and queen had hatched while designing today's game.

But there were more game surprises to come. *Crunch! Whoosh!* In the dead center of the arena, a pointed mountain abruptly shot up from somewhere below and quickly grew to rise as high as the balcony. The two centaurs had been standing at the arena's center when this happened and had to leap out of the way in a hurry.

Atop the mountain's peak stood a monstrous glow-in-the-dark creature, lit by a purple beacon.

There were excited screams and shocked gasps as everyone pointed to it. The creature was furry and black, stood on four legs, and had pointed ears. Sharp tusks curved up on either side of its snout. Clotho couldn't decide if it looked more like a pig or a bull. Either way, it was extremely scary-looking.

Snort! Snort! Flames shot from its mouth, so it also breathed fire!

A yell came from among the onlookers. "That's the Calydonian boar!" Others chimed in. "I heard that that beast likes to destroy the Calydonians' crops so they go hungry." "Yeah, and it gobbles their sheep so they don't have wool to make clothes." "And just for fun, it chases little kids to scare them!"

Atalanta nudged Clotho with an elbow. "Sounds like one wild, crazy, mean boar. The goddess of the hunt has brought forth a worthy foe, but we will beat it!"

Clotho gulped. "I'm not really skilled at fighting boars. Or anything else, for that matter. Like I told you before, I *knit*."

"Watch out, Atalanta!" Ares called down from the balcony. "That crazed boar is staring right at you. And it looks hungry!"

"Hungry? Yeah, maybe for *Meleager* meat. Because no way is it gonna gobble me or my team! I'm in this to win this," Atalanta boasted. Thus began what would later be labeled in Pheme's column THE WILD AND CRAZY CALYDONIAN BOAR HUNT.

Snort went the beast. *Stomp* went its hooves. The crowd of onlookers screamed in delicious anticipation as the monstrous creature came crashing down from its mountaintop lair. Members of both teams scattered to strategic locations around the arena in preparation for whatever the creature might do.

"Don't worry, Atalanta," Meleager yelled. "I'll save you!"

"Huh? You think I need to be saved?" scoffed Atalanta. "Take care of your own team! This is a competition, remember? I'm going to beat the boar *and* you."

Meleager looked a bit disappointed at her rebuff, but then he rallied. He seemed determined to impress her somehow, even if they were supposed to be pitted against each other, both teams vying to win the game. He shot an arrow at the boar. A miss! It angrily eyed the nearest gamers, which happened to be the two centaurs.

"Run!" the half-horse creatures shouted to each other. As the boar barreled in their direction, they galloped for the metal gate through which they'd entered the arena. But of course it had been shut

and locked. "There's no way out! We're doo-oo-oomed!" the centaurs whinny-wailed.

Lucky for them, the boar abruptly spied Atalanta. Swinging toward her, it charged. Atalanta held her ground. She drew back an arm, hefted a spear, and threw. Then, without waiting to see where the spear landed, she nocked an arrow in her bow and fired. Neither went near the boar, however. Which had been Atalanta's intent, Clotho realized a moment later. Her crafty team leader had been aiming her magic weapons at the opposite team. *Splat! Splat!* One red *X* appeared on the arm of each of Meleager's cousins, Plexippus and Toxeus. Two more each and they'd be out of the game.

Meanwhile, having caught on to what Atalanta was up to, Jason from her team threw his spear at the boar. *Zing!* Veering away from the spear—as well as Atalanta—the beast put on a burst of speed and escaped. Jason had succeeded in keeping the boar away from their team captain. However, while his attention was focused on the boar, an arrow from Meleager's bow struck him, and another from Toxeus's bow hit too. *Splat! Splat!* Red *X*s appeared on his ankle and one knee.

"Strike two!" someone in the balcony yelled, pointing at Jason.

All at once an arrow zoomed Clotho's way, shot from one of the centaurs' bows. She leaped out of its path onto a springy trampoline. *Boing!* Atalanta, who was also bouncing around to avoid an arrow, high-fived her in passing. After executing a triple somersault, Clotho came down behind a large rock. Which was coincidentally a great place to hide!

Despite her earlier misgivings, she found herself

quickly caught up in the excitement of the game. Turned out she was good at avoiding the weapons flung at her, but she felt she should also help her team somehow. Yet what could she do? She had never thrown a spear or shot an arrow in her life!

Then something struck her. (No, not an arrow or a spear, but an idea.) Since the others on her team were way more skilled with weapons than she was, she could simply offer them *her* weapons whenever they ran out of their own. So when Atalanta ran low on arrows, Clotho boinged over and fed her more. And she tossed a spear to Jason when the centaurs pinned him behind the waterfall. *Splat!* With her help, he caused a new *X* to appear on one of the centaurs.

Getting more and more involved in the action, the audience shouted (mostly) helpful suggestions to various team members. Things like "Quick! Clotho, climb that rock!" and "Meleager, splash into the waterfall from the trampoline!" and "Jason, hide in that hedge and pretend to be a topiary!"

It was tricky trying to dodge splats and boar attacks while wielding weapons at the other team. All ten players wound up dividing their attention between defeating the boar and warring with one another. Arrows and spears flew, splattering those they struck with magical red *X*s. No three-strikes-you're-out so far, though.

"Yikes!" Arachne yelled in her teeny voice as Clotho dodged yet another arrow. "I thought coming along with you would be an adventure. But this is freaking me out!"

"Hush!" Clotho replied. "I need to concentrate, or I'll get *X*-ed! Maybe you should've stayed in my bag. Or better yet, back at your shop!"

Splat! An arrow smacked Euphemus on Atalanta's team. His first *X*. Then, in quick succession, two more arrows struck him. Three strikes! Immediately, a trap door in the floor opened up under the boy's feet. It stayed open just long enough for him to fall downward and away through a chute. Then the trap door disappeared without a trace. Once he was gone, Atalanta's team had one less member. Which meant they were down to four now.

Apparently growing terrified at all the action going on around them, Arachne waved her skinny legs in the air. "Yoo-hoo!" she shouted to the other team. "We give up! Don't splat us."

"Stop it!" Clotho demanded. "You're attracting attention. You're going to get us paint-bombed!"

Arachne's eyes lit up. "Hey, good thinking. I've changed my mind. If the only way out of this arena is

to get triple *X*s, we should actually *try* to get splatted!"

"No way!" Clotho replied. "No one else is trying to lose on purpose to escape the arena. I refuse to either."

Throughout the game Meleager had kept a protective eye on his new crush, Atalanta. Which posed a problem for his team. When the boar charged her while she was aiming at the centaurs on Meleager's team, he chose to help her instead of them. Ducking behind a large rock, he aimed at the boar and called out to her, "Run, girl!" *Zing!* The boar veered away and his shot missed.

The centaurs frowned. "*Hey!* What about us? We're your teammates. You should help us, not her!"

"Yeah! This *young woman* can protect *herself*, dude!" Atalanta informed Meleager, cocking a

thumb at her chest. "Besides, I'm a way better shot than you." So saying, she planted her sandaled feet wide and fired off two arrows from her bow, catching the centaurs off guard. *Zing! Zing!*

"Hey!" "Rats!" they yelled in disappointment as her red *X*s splatted them. Since these were their third strikes each, trap doors opened beneath them. *Whoosh!* With identical expressions of surprise on their faces, both tumbled downward and away.

"Score!" shouted Atalanta, punching her bow high. She turned her aim toward Meleager then, but he'd already bounced away on a trampoline. On his team, only he and his two cousins remained now. Atalanta's team still had four.

Minutes later, during a brief pause in the action, Clotho saw that the centaurs and Euphemus were now back upstairs on the balcony. They'd joined those at the railing to watch the ongoing battle. Since all who'd struck out seemed unharmed, she guessed they had met with a soft landing when they'd fallen through the arena floor. There must be pads down there, and a staircase that led back up to the balcony. *Phew! Good to know!*

She ducked as Meleager's cousins doubled down on their offense, firing in many directions. In no time at all Theseus from Team Atalanta wore two *X*s. Suddenly the boar managed to headbutt him into a high, wild somersault, causing a third *X* to appear on his rear end. Apparently, a headbutt equaled being splatted with an arrow or spear in this game. When Theseus reached the arena floor again, a trap door opened under him and he disappeared. *Whoosh!*

Only three were left on each team now, counting both captains.

Splat! Jason was hit a third time, and gone from the game. Now it was down to three against two. Meleager and his cousins against Atalanta and Clotho. And the boar against them all! Clotho could hardly believe she had managed to survive so far.

The teams continued on the offense, chasing the Calydonian boar around and around a huge shape-shifting rock until the boar reversed course to chase *them*! Tired at last, it hid in some scraggly bushes.

Clotho got caught up in the action, bouncing around from one trampoline to another. Arrows and spears flew. It was total chaos! A free-for-all!

"Any advice, Athena and Heracles?" Atalanta called up to the bleachers as she took cover behind a topiary shaped like a giant rabbit. "Didn't you guys capture a boar once?"

"Yeah, the Erymanthian boar," Heracles shouted down to her.

"It was a talking boar, though," Athena added. "So we were able to trick it into visiting Heracles' cousin, who had to listen to it tell its favorite long, boring stories because he was trapped in a vase. I doubt that will work with this boar, unfortunately."

"Blah blah blah," Arachne muttered from Clotho's shoulder as Clotho boinged from a flower-shaped trampoline onto a snowflake-shaped one. "What a show-off. That Athena thinks she's *sooo* clever." In spite of the revenge Athena had visited upon her, Arachne had obviously not learned a lesson about giving due respect to immortals!

"You shouldn't say such things. Besides, I think Athena's nice," Clotho told the mouthy spider. Luckily, Arachne's voice was tiny, and the sounds of the fighting were loud. No one else seemed to have heard her latest insult.

Moments later Atalanta found a clear shot at the boar. *Zing!* Her arrow glanced off its nose. *Splat!* She tried another. *Zing!* Another splat! And the boar's ear fell off and hit the ground with a metallic-sounding *clank*.

Metallic-sounding? What was up with that? wondered Clotho. Then it dawned on her. The boar wasn't real! She clapped a hand to her forehead. *Duh!* A real boar would endanger the lives of the players. And using a real boar would also be animal cruelty! So this boar must be only a mechanical representation of the famous Calydonian boar, created for this game.

Two red *X*s appeared on the boar's side. "Two strikes! One more, you dumb ol' boar; then your bacon will be mine," crowed Atalanta.

The boar turned. Eyes on her, it pawed the ground. Then, snorting with rage, it charged!

Atalanta quickly nocked a new arrow in her bow. But before she could fire it off, Meleager leaped toward her and elbowed her out of the way.

"Go hide while I handle this!" he commanded. *Zing!* He heaved his spear and broadsided the approaching boar. *Splat!* A third red *X* appeared on its side. The beast went up in a puff of smoke. And in its place there now stood a dazzling, jeweled, boar-shaped trophy!

8
Tricked!

SUDDENLY THE MUSICAL NOTES OF A LUTE sounded in the arena. The king had said that the sound of a lute would signal: Game over!

"Yay, Team Meleager! We have the most players left on our team. We won!" yelled Plexippus and Toxeus. They bumped fists and held the trophy high in triumph. Their joy was short-lived, however.

They and everyone else were astonished to see

Meleager suddenly grab the trophy and go down on bended knee before Atalanta. He held it out to her. "As a token of my esteem, I award this trophy to you," he told her.

A hush fell over the arena, bleachers, and balcony. Atalanta hesitated for a moment, but then she accepted the trophy. "Uh, thanks."

"Wait! Our team won. Why should *she* get the prize?" protested Plexippus.

"Yeah! No fair," complained Toxeus.

Meleager huffed. "I'm the team captain, so we play by my rules. What I say goes!"

Huh? Clotho could guess how Meleager's cousins must feel. Too often she'd been bossed around in the name of rules she'd had no part in making. By her sisters. And Zeus, too! Maybe finally disobeying his no-hanging-with-mortals rule today had made her rebellious. Because she was starting to think that everyone should get to have input on rules that affected them—in most cases, anyway.

Before she could suggest that Meleager talk things over with his cousins and listen to their objections, the prince turned his bow and arrow on the two boys. *Zing! Zing!* He splatted them both!

They had been tagged twice already, so when a third red *X* appeared on Toxeus's elbow and a third one on Plexippus's chest, they were done for. *Whoosh!* They were whisked away through trap doors.

The crowd on the balcony responded to Meleager's betrayal of his own team members with stunned silence. As if to make clear that the game was now officially over, however, the arena's metal exit gate clanked and swung itself open.

Quickly Clotho, Atalanta, and Meleager took off their battle gear and put their sandals back on. Clotho slung the straps of her travel bag over her shoulder as all three hurried back up the ramp. While making their way to the balcony, they could hear the murmurs of astonishment begin to rise from the onlookers there.

"Can you believe it?" Clotho heard Apollo say.

"No! I mean, he shot his *own team members* out of the game!" Poseidon exclaimed.

"Yeah! And he gave their trophy to the competition!" Ares said, sounding disgusted as well as bewildered.

Up on the balcony again at last, Clotho was just in time to hear Artemis say, "Atalanta deserved it. I mean, she got in the most shots at the boar. Two to Meleager's one."

"Yeah, I think it's sweet that he wanted her to have the trophy," said Aphrodite.

Athena leaned over to Artemis. "Hey! Speaking of that boar, I just now got what you meant when you warned us that this game would be a little *boring*. You meant BOAR-ing!"

Artemis grinned. "Hephaestus made that replica of the Calydonian boar for me out of some magical metal in his blacksmith shop back at Mount Olympus Academy. No matter how many times it's splatted out of the arena at the end of a game, it'll return again to play another one when summoned. That godboy is amazingly skilled."

Now that the game had finally ended, members of both teams seemed to have accepted the unusual outcome. All were being good sports about it. They were being celebrated as heroes of the day for having performed in the first game ever in the arena. Even Plexippus and Toxeus were clapping others on their backs in high spirits.

Although Meleager still seemed to be crushing on Atalanta, following her around like a little lost puppy, she was doing her best to ignore him. Finally, however, she lost her patience. She cupped a hand to her ear and said to him, "I think I hear the king and queen calling you." When he turned to look for his parents, she slipped out of Game On!, taking the trophy with her.

Meleager drooped when he realized she'd tricked him, but then perked up again when Heracles came over to talk to him. Clotho wondered if Meleager would ever come to regret handing his team's trophy over to Atalanta. Or maybe he was just happy to have done something that made her smile.

"Kitten snacks?" said Arachne's tiny voice, reminding Clotho of her plan to get food for the kitten they'd left back at the shop in the IM. Over at the snack table Clotho quickly found a takeaway container, put some tuna sandwiches and other kitten-friendly tidbits inside it, and stowed it in her bag. With the spider still riding on her shoulder, she was about to sneak out to the atrium when the king produced a new surprise.

"Another Calydonian Boar Hunt game will begin tomorrow," he announced to the crowd. "So do return, MOA students. You might just be chosen to play! And with the added excitement of your immortal abilities, mortals will surely want to be in the audience."

"Every game, every day, will be slightly different, so expect the unexpected," the queen added with a wink.

Nodding, the king continued. "Over the coming weeks, a half-dozen more games will be added. They'll rotate in and out of our three-sectioned arena."

"We think you'll enjoy all the thrilling, action-packed excitement we've planned. Take a look at this preview of just one of those new games, which opens tomorrow!" the queen called out.

With that the king pulled a cord hanging from the ceiling. This opened the curtain that hid a second pizza-slice-shaped area of the arena. *Whoosh!*

Clotho was drawn to the railing to discover what had been revealed. To her surprise, Hades and Persephone were hard at work down in the arena, hanging a sign over what looked to be a new game. Popping up from their task, both were obviously startled to find so many eyes on them. This must be the secret project Persephone had mentioned in Cassandra's bakery earlier that morning!

"Ta-da!" boomed the king, gesturing grandly

toward the pair. "As you can see, Persephone and Hades are finishing up the creation of our second game even now: Tartarus Two, the Underworld."

The goddessgirl and godboy smiled and waved up at the crowd in the balcony. It seemed that Persephone hadn't gone to help Hades in the *real* Underworld as Athena and Aphrodite had thought. Instead, she'd been helping him create an Underworld *game* here in the IM.

Looks interesting, thought Clotho, leaning as far as she could over the railing to peer down. She spotted a large pool with fruit trees nearby, a river of lava, lots of rocks, and clumps of white flowers. Asphodel, she knew: flowers that grew throughout the Underworld.

Pheme had been standing near Clotho at the railing. Now she whipped out a notescroll and feather pen and called down to Persephone and Hades.

"Tell us about Tartarus Two. I'll write an article about it for *Teen Scrollazine*."

Persephone's green eyes lit with excitement. "Well, as everyone knows, only the truly evil wind up being punished in the real Tartarus down in the Underworld. It's the deepest, scariest, gloomiest place ever! In Tartarus Two, players will be banished to our pretend Tartarus here for various silly reasons and will then have to try to escape fun yet puzzling punishments to get themselves out."

"Sheesh, immortals just love punishing people, right?" Arachne grumbled.

"You heard what Artemis read from her Revenge-ology scroll: When a mortal insults a god or goddess, retribution is required," Clotho replied quietly so as not to be overheard. "So maybe you're lucky Athena didn't send you to the real Tartarus after that tapestry you made poking fun at Zeus. By making you a spider, at least her punishment allowed you to still be able to weave your webs."

Arachne appeared to consider that for a moment, one leg scratching her body. "Whatever," she muttered. She spun out a long thread from Clotho's shoulder down to her travel bag and ducked inside it.

Clotho turned to go, but stopped when she felt a sharp pull on her hair. "Ow!" Looking down, she saw that a lock of her long black hair had somehow gotten tangled around the balcony railing. As she untangled it, an image of a knotted, tangled thread floating skyward formed in her mind.

Huh? Before she could decide what this could mean, a strange, glittery breeze swirled onto the balcony, bringing a papyrus scroll with it. "I come from Mount Olympus with a message for the Fates

from Zeus himself!" the wind howled. "Fates, are you present?"

Uh-oh, thought Clotho, going pale. Zeus knew she was here? Since his message wasn't addressed to her in particular, he must think her sisters were here as well. What could he want? Had he heard that she'd been mingling with mortals? Was he angry? Did he have punishment on his mind? *Yikes!*

"The Fates?" Pandora echoed, sounding awed. "Here?" Everyone looked around, murmuring excitedly. Picturing the instant complaint party that might begin if Pandora or any other mortals found out she was the one the magic breeze was looking for (well, *one* of the ones), Clotho ducked her head. Eyeing the exit, she began to edge away through the crowd. She couldn't let the messagescroll find her! But then she heard something that stopped her in her tracks.

"The Fates aren't so smart. I know for a fact that my mom tricked them." It was Meleager, and he was boasting to Ares, Poseidon, and Apollo. The four boys were standing right behind her.

"Oh yeah? How'd your mom do that?" Poseidon demanded to know. Clotho stood as if frozen, eavesdropping (while pretending not to).

"Well . . . I'm not supposed to tell," Prince Meleager admitted in a low voice. It was obvious to her that he wanted to impress the godboys, though. He leaned in closer. "My mom says that when I was born, she dreamed that my Thread of Fate was tangled and knotted."

Clotho's forehead wrinkled as a long-ago memory tugged at her. *Tangle. Meleager.* Suddenly her brain connected the dots. That Thread of Fate she'd tangled twelve years ago? It had been his!

"In my mom's dream, the three Fates told her that my destiny was to die as soon as a log burning in our fireplace turned to ashes," Meleager went on. "So my mom simply removed the log before it could burn up. And here I am, still alive. Easy-peasy!"

Ares folded his arms over his chest, appearing skeptical. "No way! The Fates can't be tricked like that."

Meleager placed a hand over his heart. "True story. On my honor."

Argh! thought Clotho. Her sisters had always warned that if she broke even one rule—in this case the rule against stopping partway through the telling of a fate years ago—it would have consequences. They'd been right. It had been an accident, but still.

And here at the IM today, she'd broken Rule #3 big-time by hanging out with numerous mortals *on purpose*. She shuddered to think what unexpected consequences might come from that.

Feeling confused, and wanting to keep the messagescroll from finding her, Clotho scurried off. Had Zeus discovered her twelve-year-old mistake? Was that what his messagescroll for the Fates was all about? *Gulp!* When the strange breeze whooshed it closer, she put on a burst of speed and zoomed away from it.

Not watching where she was going, she accidentally bumped into a mortal boy. "Ow," he cried out, hopping around. "You stepped on my toe!" It was that boy she'd seen earlier in the green cape.

"I'm so sorry. 'Scuse me," she threw the words over her shoulder at him as she dashed for the exit.

Seconds later, she was pushing through the door into Arachne's shop again. First thing, she checked for the kitten. It wasn't there. But when she called,

"Here, kitty, kitty!" it came scampering in through the hole in the wall she'd discovered before. She scraped the tuna from the little sandwiches she'd brought onto a plate and set that, the other snacks, and a bowl of fresh water on the kitchenette floor. That adorable sweetie pie quickly gobbled up every morsel. *Aww!*

It had only just finished when all at once the shop door began to rattle. With a startled hiss, the kitten dove into a basket of yarn to hide as the door whooshed open. The determined breeze carrying that messagescroll whisked inside. Clotho watched in dismay as it whirled around the shop, sending yarn balls and spools of ribbon rolling across the floor. Scissors and shears hanging on the pegboard swayed in its wake, clinking together like wind chimes.

Somehow this breeze had found her! She pressed

her back to the wall and watched it approach. "Art thou a Fate?" it asked.

Even if she could escape the shop, it would probably track her down again. So, reluctantly, she admitted, "Mm-hm. Clotho."

The breeze stilled, causing the scroll it carried to drop at her feet. "Finally! I have been looking everywhere. Zeus wasn't sure where any of you'd be. His instructions to me were to wait until you read his message and give me a reply," it informed her.

Left no choice, Clotho picked up the scroll. *Pzzt!* "Ow!" It buzzed her fingertips with an electric charge. A sure sign it had come from that thunderbolty Zeus! She unrolled it with dread and began to silently read.

Hello, Fates,

It's your lucky day! Because you are invited to the Immortal Marketplace tomorrow at noon to help celebrate my birthday!

A smile of relief spread over Clotho's face. This was no reprimand. It was an invitation! Hooray! She read on:

The IM will close for a few hours, so don't worry, no chance of you rubbing elbows with any more mortals than necessary as per my Rule #3. So be there or be square.

Yours in thunder,

Zeus

P.S. Bring presents

Below his P.S., Zeus had drawn pictures of what she guessed were gift suggestions. It was hard to tell exactly what the pictures represented, however. One looked like a silly mustache and lips. Or more likely a thunderbolt with a festive bow on it? And was the drawing beside that one a birdhouse or a helmet? And what was up with the hairy bracelets below that? Wait, no. Maybe those were supposed to be olive wreaths?

Zeus was a mighty powerful guy, but he was also *mighty* bad at art. Which Clotho actually appreciated, because it wouldn't be fair if he were great at everything!

"What does the messagescroll say?" Arachne demanded to know. The spider had crawled out of Clotho's bag and up the wall to begin weaving new webs in a high corner of the stairwell next to the kitchenette. When Clotho explained about the invitation, Arachne let out an excited squeak. "*Party?* Tomorrow? Ooh! Take me with you, please, please, please?"

"You want to go?" Clotho asked in surprise. She set the scroll on a nearby counter, then began going around putting everything the breeze had disturbed back where it belonged. "I thought you didn't like immortals."

Arachne did another one of her bug shrugs—er, *arachnid* shrugs. "Whatever," she replied. "But I do like parties. There's always food, which might attract flies, which are my kind of snacks. I mean, flies are so dumb. I just have to sit on my web and wait for them to fly into it and get stuck. Instant meal. *Yum*-mee!" The spider rubbed two legs together in gleeful anticipation.

"Well?" the magic breeze huff-puffed at Clotho. It

was still awaiting a reply to the invitation, she realized.

"Oh! Yes, please tell Zeus I'll be at the party, thanks," she said. Then she quickly added, "I don't think my sisters can make it, though."

She hated to leave out her sisters. Still, she couldn't take the chance of Lachesis and Atropos finding out from anyone at the party that she'd been mingling with mortals. Nor did she want them to hear any talk about how Meleager's mom had managed to trick the Fates. They'd be so upset, they'd never let her hear the end of it! She only hoped Zeus didn't learn about any of that stuff either.

Like most everyone, Zeus thought of the Fates as a single unit, instead of as three individuals. If he did find out about her rule breaking or her Meleager mistake, it wouldn't be fair if her sisters wound up sharing the blame. So that was another reason—an *un*selfish one—to keep mum about the invitation.

She knew she'd better attend, however. Because when the King of the Gods invites you and your sisters to his birthday party, at least one of you had better show up to represent the rest if you know what's good for you.

"I will relay your message," replied the breeze. In a swirl of magic, it departed through the shop's open door. As soon as it was gone, Clotho dashed over to the bottom step of the stairs to grab her bag. Remembering she still wore the Game On! button, she pulled it off and set it aside. She needed to gather the wool and yarn she'd come to the IM to get, and scram before she broke any more Zeus rules!

But she screeched to a halt when she heard a new voice say, "So are you the Fate that scroll was looking for?"

9
Tantalus

CLOTHO JUMPED AROUND. JUST INSIDE THE shop doorway stood the spiky-haired, green-caped mortal boy. The same one whose foot she had sort of trampled while leaving Game On!

"What do you want?" she asked cautiously.

Grinning at her, he said, "I followed that magic breeze over here from Game On! and snuck in. Heard everything, including what you told that

spider." Lifting his chin in Arachne's direction, he moseyed farther into the shop. He looked around and then eyed Clotho again. "I'm Tantalus. And you're Clotho? So are you really one of the Fates? How come your skin doesn't shimmer like other immortals'?"

Thunk! Clotho dropped her bag on the bottom step again. It tipped on its side, causing some of her animal finger puppets to tumble out as she stared hard at him. *Tantalus.* His name was strangely familiar to her. But why?

"Hey, girl! Snap out of it," Arachne prodded when Clotho didn't reply fast enough to suit her. "Answer the boy's questions."

Clotho shot a frown at Arachne. "I think I'm starting to get why Athena turned you into a bug."

"Arachnid! Arachnid! How many times do I have

to tell you?" complained the spider, rolling all eight of her eyes. Pouting now, Arachne crawled to a dark corner and began spinning a new web to which she'd probably add more insults to the gods and goddesses—Clotho included!

Tantalus didn't appear startled to hear a spider talking. Why? Because he'd been sneakily listening the whole time he'd been here, as he'd already admitted.

"Okay, yes," Clotho told him. "I am a Fate. Our skin isn't glittery on purpose so we won't be recognized. We're not allowed to draw mortals' attention or hang out with you guys at all."

Tantalus's head jerked back in surprise. "But you just played a game with some mortals at Game On!" he reminded her. "Isn't that 'hanging out'?"

Clotho gave him a weak smile. To avoid having to

answer that question, she changed the subject. "So, anyway, I don't mean to be rude or anything, but I really need to gather some craft stuff and get going. Also, this is Arachne's shop, so I shouldn't be letting random people in to bother her. Which means you should probably get going too." To emphasize her request, she made shooing motions toward the door.

"He can stay awhile. I don't mind," Arachne chimed in unhelpfully.

"So . . . does Zeus know you're the Fate who messed up Meleager's destiny?" Tantalus asked Clotho.

Her mouth dropped open. "How'd you know that?"

Tantalus crossed his arms and smirked. "Ha! I didn't till you just now confirmed it. I heard some godboys talking about it back in Game On! But I figured there was no way Meleager's mom could've fixed his destiny so easily by removing that burning log. Not unless one of you Fates had made a mistake in spinning his Thread of Fate to begin with. So you're the spinner?"

Clotho hesitated, and then sighed. "Okay, yeah, you got me. My job is to read the names on the Destiny List and spin the Threads of Fate. Twelve years ago, I accidentally tangled and knotted Meleager's thread."

In her mind's eye she recalled watching Meleager's thread drift toward the heavens. Saw it come into contact with the thread of the boy whose name had come before his on the Destiny List.

Her eyes went wide. So that was why she remembered Tantalus's name! It had been his thread that had briefly touched Meleager's. What did it mean

that both boys had come together at Game On! today? Had she caused their destinies to be bound up in some way she wasn't aware of?

She decided to dig for information. "So how do you know Prince Meleager?" she asked, trying to sound casual.

"I don't. I heard about Game On! opening. That's the only reason I came to the IM." Tantalus tapped a fingertip on his cheek. He seemed to momentarily turn deep inside his own thoughts. "A knotted, tangled thread, huh? Interesting," he mused. "I didn't think Fates, or any immortals, ever made mistakes."

"Well, we try not to, and we fix the ones we make if we can," she told him honestly.

His eyes shone with glee, and maybe a bit of spite? "Ha! Which means you do make them! So

high-and-mighty immortals are not any better than mortals when it comes to mistakes?"

Clotho let out a groan. "Don't let any other goddesses or gods hear you say that. That kind of talk makes us immortals cranky."

"I can vouch for that!" Arachne piped up from her corner. Then she began to mumble grumpily. "Horrible Athena . . . turned me into a spider . . . said the tapestry I wove insulted the gods . . . some people can't take a joke."

"Yeah, well, as jokes go, insults are not particularly funny to immortals," Clotho informed both the spider and Tantalus.

Her gaze narrowed on the boy. "Please promise me you won't tell anyone what I've told you or what you overheard. It could get my sisters and me in big trouble with Zeus. In fact, just forget you ever met me and that we ever had this discussion, okay?"

Before Tantalus had a chance to answer, Clotho heard Athena's voice. "The door's open," that goddessgirl said to whoever was with her. She sounded surprised by this as she stepped inside the shop. Aphrodite, Artemis, and Medusa entered behind her. "Told you I saw that magic breeze fly toward this shop," Medusa said.

Noticing Clotho and Tantalus, the four girls moved their way. Athena spied Zeus's messagescroll on the counter and put two and two together. "You're the Fate the magic breeze was looking for?" she asked Clotho in surprise.

Ye gods! They didn't call Athena a brain for nothing. With a groan, Clotho nodded and then dropped her head into the palm of her hand. So much for keeping her true identity secret from these girls.

"And who are you?" Aphrodite asked Tantalus. Bedazzled by her beauty, as boys often were, he went speechless for a few moments. By the time he finally recovered and was introducing himself, Clotho looked up to see that the dozen snakes on Medusa's head had begun flicking their tongues at Arachne. The spider let out a shriek and zoomed up a silky web strand to hide on the ceiling out of their reach.

Abruptly remembering the THEENY IS A MEANIE! and ZEUS IS A GOOSE! insults woven into Arachne's webs, Clotho leaped into action. She grabbed a broom and swept any offensively worded cobwebs away before anyone—especially Athena—could read them. Although Arachne could be annoying, Clotho didn't really want her to get in so much trouble that she wound up banished to the real Tartarus!

Once the webs were gone, she saw that the girls

and Tantalus were looking at her a little oddly. Somewhat embarrassed, she set the broom aside. "Um. Just cleaning up a little. I, er, have never been to the Immortal Marketplace, but I saw this shop and wandered in hoping to find some wool and yarn. Don't want to leave a mess."

"Hey! You were on Atalanta's team in Game On!, weren't you?" Artemis realized just then. "Clotho, right? You and Atalanta did good work. Go, girl power!" she added, punching a fist in the air.

"Thanks, it was fun," said Clotho, pleased by the compliment. Kneeling by the steps, she began gathering her scattered finger puppets and stuffing them back in her bag. She'd just grab some yarn and wool and get going.

"Hey! Those look a lot like the finger puppets we saw at Cassandra's," noted Aphrodite, pointing

at the puppets clutched in Clotho's arms.

She and the other girls came closer. "Did you make them? And leave some of them in the Oracle-O Bakery?" asked Athena. She picked up an owl puppet Clotho had missed from the stair, popped it on her finger, and wiggled it close to her own face, grinning.

Clotho nodded. "Yeah, I did. You can keep that one if you want. Because owls are kind of your symbol, right?"

"Wow, thanks!" said Athena, looking delighted. "Hey! You know who would love these?" she added, glancing at her friends.

"Meow, meow . . . Zeus?" Aphrodite asked in a high squeaky voice. She had nabbed a kitten puppet from the floor and was wiggling it on her index finger. Hearing her pretend meows, the shop kitten popped its head up from the basket where it had hidden.

"Exactly!" said Athena. Looking over at Clotho, she explained, "My dad is always playing with my baby sister Hebe's toys." Her eyes turned affectionate. "He's like a little kid sometimes. It's his birthday tomorrow, and he's giving a big, festive luncheon here at the Immortal Marketplace."

"I know, I'm going. That messagescroll I got from him was an invitation," said Clotho.

"Nice! I was just thinking that these puppets would make great party favors," said Athena, her blue-gray eyes sparkling. "I really like knitting, but I don't know these patterns. Could you possibly show us how to make some for him and all the guests?"

Clotho blinked at her, really wanting to agree. But she made herself shake her head no to avoid

any more rule-breaking mingling. "Sorry, gotta go. You're welcome to just take all the puppets I've already made, though. You could add little decorations to personalize them and make them special. There are all kinds of sequins and beads and other things like that in this shop you could use."

Remembering that it wasn't her place to make this offer, Clotho glanced over at Arachne to get her reaction. Surprisingly, Arachne nodded yes. She was getting the feeling this spider was lonely. So lonely that she was willing to keep her nemesis Athena and her friends here decorating party favors if only for their company.

"You're going to give *finger puppets* to everyone at Zeus's party?" scoffed a new voice. It sounded like Poseidon. The girls whirled around to see that he, Ares, and Apollo had entered the shop too, and overheard.

"Sure, why not?" said Aphrodite.

Ares came over to study the puppets Clotho held. To her surprise he said, "I want to decorate some. Will you show me how?"

"Dude," said Poseidon, shaking his head. "You have no talent for doing creative stuff. Remember that scabbard you tried to sew for your sword that one time? It looked like a very, very sad boa constrictor. Sorry, but no. Just *no*."

"Hey, it's for Zeus! I'm up for trying. With a little effort, I think we could transform these puppets into some killer hero-type creatures," argued Ares.

Poseidon just sighed.

Finally Tantalus spoke up, introducing himself to

the godboys and adding, "You know what would be mega-cool? If we put on a finger-puppet show for Zeus. A battle or something awesome like that. Are ya with me?"

Huh? thought Clotho. Judging from Tantalus's delight in immortal mistakes, she wouldn't have thought he'd be interested in helping them do something nice for Zeus's birthday. Seemed she was wrong.

"Yeah! Maybe reenact the Titan-Olympian war with animal puppets," enthused Apollo. "We could make it super exciting. Plus we could add some humor, and maybe some songs from Heavens Above, too!" That was the name of his band, Clotho knew.

"But mostly lots of battles and pillaging!" said Ares, fist-bumping with Apollo and Artemis.

Though Poseidon had pooh-poohed the idea

of Ares decorating puppets, he'd perked up at Tantalus's show suggestion. "Now you're talking. I'm in," he told the others.

"Ooh! Olympian puppets battling Titan puppets? My dad will go crazy for that. So perfect!" said Athena, bouncing on her toes and clapping.

"I'm not that good at sewing and crafty stuff," Medusa told Clotho, wrinkling her nose. "So maybe you and Athena could help the rest of us? Since you're both good at that kind of thing?"

When Athena nodded, Clotho found herself doing the same. "Well, okay, I guess maybe I could stay and get you started." Zeus had invited her to his party, right? she reasoned. He must know she'd meet some of these other kids there anyway, so . . . She glanced through the kitchenette window at a sundial outside the IM. "It's only one o'clock, and I just remembered I don't have to be anywhere till nightfall."

"Mega-cool," Athena went on. "Since many of us here fought in the war, I'm thinking some of the puppets should probably be representations of us, only in cute animal form."

"Ooh! That's clever!" said Clotho.

Aphrodite nodded enthusiastically. "We'll need twenty-four combatants—twelve Olympians and twelve Titans."

"Can you show me how to turn one of those puppets into a shark-shaped version of me?" Poseidon asked Clotho eagerly.

"Oh! I love dogs! Can you help me turn these into Titans for our play?" added Artemis, holding up three cute little dog puppets Clotho had made a while ago.

Clotho grinned at her. "Sure!" Quickly she gathered up all the little puppets that had spilled on the steps, plus the ones that remained in her bag. As she set them out on a worktable, her enthusiasm for the idea of sharing her skills grew.

"You guys can pick any of these to decorate or alter however you want," she went on. "I don't have a pattern for my puppets, but I promised a, uh, friend in Colchis that I'd drop off some serpent puppets one day soon. So I'll make one of those now to show you some puppet-knitting basics, in case you want to make your own new characters for tomorrow's show."

Quickly she gave knitting lessons to those who wanted to add arms, legs, hair, little outfits, battle gear, and other stuff to their already-made animal puppets. The others watched carefully as she showed them how to create a puppet from scratch, using serpents as her example. Then everyone set to work. There was much laughter as the goddess-girls, godboys, and Tantalus and Medusa knitted, wove, glued, and got creative. Now and then they slid puppets onto their fingers and made them have silly conversations.

Sometime later, Ares announced, "I'm naming mine Skunktastic Ares. Its superpower is going to be its stink ray." He held up his index finger to show off a black-and-white skunk puppet of Clotho's to which he had added big muscles. Unfortunately, his alterations had made it looked more like a rat than a skunk. Still, he got an *E* for effort, and the puppet did look sort of heroic.

Aphrodite reworked Clotho's kitten puppet into one with a pink sequined collar with bright blue

eyes, dubbing it AphroCatty. With some time left over, she also knitted a spear for Ares's skunk.

"Look what I made!" Apollo called out after a while. He whipped his hand up from behind his back to show everyone the puppet Clotho had helped him knit. With a body shaped like a silver thunderbolt, it had meaty arms. Apollo had decorated it with a thick red beard and hair, and glued-on googly eyeballs. He'd made the puppet extra-large, requiring two fingers to move it. "Ta-da! Thunder-Zeus!" he announced to grins and cheers.

"And I made a Crabby-Cronus!" Medusa crowed, perching the crablike puppet she'd created on a finger. Cronus was the grumpy king of the Titans. He'd be pitted directly against Zeus in their puppet show.

"This puppet represents me. So I'm naming it Owlthena!" announced Athena. With additional

decorations, she had transformed Clotho's little brown owl puppet into something magnificently adorable. She'd added two large blue-gray sequins to make eyes that matched the color of hers, a triangle-shaped bead for an owl-like nose, and flowing brown yarn for hair. Also some teeny fake feathers on each wing. The puppet really looked a little bit like her now, except maybe for the beaky nose and feathers.

Tantalus had made a boy-shaped puppet of ivory-colored yarn instead of an animal. "I think I'll call him Pelops. Because he's lopsided and always 'plops' over on my finger. He's not one of the Titans or Olympians, but I figure he can be the narrator of our puppet show," he told the others.

He then held up a large wooden box full of yarn, about five feet square. "Let's dump out this yarn and cut out the back of this box so it's open front to back.

We can add a little paint and make it into our puppet theater."

As everyone continued to work, Arachne watched from her web, uncomplaining for once. Clotho could almost swear the spider wore a smile on her face.

Clotho found herself smiling too as she helped Artemis transform her floppy-eared dogs into Titan characters. She had never, ever hung out with anyone except her sisters until today. This was fu-un!

The little white shop kitten was enjoying a lot of attention too, she saw. Now and then, she or the others took breaks to play with it or let it cuddle in their laps. Once, she glanced over to see that Poseidon had tied a piece of yarn to the end of his trident and was dangling it for the kitten to chase.

After they'd all finished making puppets and the theater, they came up with a simple, short, and silly show that didn't take long to perfect. Naturally, it was decided that the twelve Olympians would fight the twelve Titans as had actually happened in the real battle. And no question the Olympians would emerge victorious.

At the last minute, the group decided to add red capes to all the Titan puppets and blue capes to all the Olympians. This would help the audience easily tell who was who and know who to root for during the battles. Tantalus added a green cape to his puppet, since it would be the narrator, not part of the actual show.

Clotho could hardly believe how fast the time inside the shop passed as they all joked around and worked. Sooner than she would've liked, the fist-size fluffy pom-poms on her magic sandals began to spin around like whirlybirds. The kitten immedi-

ately pounced on the pom-poms, thinking they were new toys or maybe birds. Everyone else stared at her whirling pom-poms in surprise.

"They're on a timer," Clotho explained. "To remind me when it's time to go meet my sisters. We spin the Threads of Fate for newborns on the Destiny List every night. So I've got to get going."

After the group agreed to meet at Game On! the next morning before the party to set up and rehearse their play one last time, Clotho quickly ushered everyone out. She stayed behind just long enough to give the kitten a quick good-bye cuddle. "See you tomorrow, sweetie pie," she told it. Then she, too, headed for the door.

Arachne's voice followed her. "So will everyone be returning?" Clotho looked back over her shoulder. Grinning and pointing a finger at the spider, she said, "Ha! Admit it. You liked us hanging out in your shop, didn't you? You enjoyed our company—both mortals *and* immortals!"

The spider gave a shrug. "Well . . . I still think immortals are annoying," Arachne said. "But it *was* a lot more exciting around here than usual."

If Arachne liked company, was it possible she'd be okay with Clotho coming here to work some days? She would try to avoid being seen by mortals each time she came, of course, so that she wouldn't keep breaking the "no mingling" rule. Still, hanging out with the spider, they'd both be a little less lonely, right?

No time to talk about this now, though, since she needed to get going. So for the moment Clotho simply nodded. "Yeah, we'll be back tomorrow morning to pick up everything for the party and take it over to Game On! I'll give you a ride there if you still want to go."

"Yes!" said the spider. Then, seeming a little embarrassed about her enthusiasm, Arachne added, "Not that I care that much either way. Whatever."

Clotho hid a smile. "A word of advice," she said to the spider on her way out. "Cool it with weaving the web insults tomorrow. You don't want to get in trouble . . . again."

10

Orion's Belt

ONCE OUTSIDE THE IMMORTAL MARKETPLACE, Clotho lifted off in her magic sandals. She skimmed across the ground at first, then flew upward, moving ever higher to go meet her sisters for another night of work.

Although she was weighed down by worries about her twelve-year-old mistakes with Meleager and Tantalus, as well as the possibility that Zeus might

discover she'd broken his mortal-mingling rule, her physical load was lighter than usual. Because tonight her travel bag held only her distaff, her spindle, and a bag of sheep's wool. With Arachne's permission, she'd left her other belongings at the sewing shop overnight.

Quickly she instructed her sandals:

"Up and away to Orion.
Go where my sisters are.
Find that constellation's belt
And land me on a star."

Already the sun was going down and Nyx was beginning to spread her blue-black star-studded cape to envelop the heavens. When that goddessgirl of night flung the Orion constellation into the sky,

its seven stars moved into position, shaping a hunter holding a bow and arrow.

"Thanks for the starry night!" Clotho called with a wave. Nyx's hands were busily working her cape, but she sent a bright smile. "You're welcome!" she called back in return.

Hair streaming behind her in the wind, Clotho headed straight for the trio of stars that made up Orion's Belt. By the time she reached the constellation, her sisters were already sitting on the first two of them, Alnilam and Mintaka. Clotho did the triple somersault she'd perfected earlier at Game On! and landed to sit on Alnitak, the belt's third star.

"Wow, little sis, are you going out for gymnastics or something?" said Lachesis, her olive-green eyes twinkling merrily.

Atropos raised an eyebrow. "Yeah, where'd you

learn such awesome acrobatics? What's up, anyway?"

Not wanting to reveal news of her trip to the IM and her participation in today's game, Clotho simply shrugged. Then she gestured at the millions of stars surrounding them and the Earth far below. "You ask what's up?" she said to Atropos. "Well, *we* are! Can't get much more *up* than the stars, right?"

To her delight her sisters laughed. Though she longed for a home of her own, Clotho did like visiting amazing sights like Orion up close. It was a treat few would ever get the chance to enjoy. Even if they eventually got a home, nothing would prevent them from still venturing out to fab new places like this to work sometimes.

"So you found some wool," Lachesis noted. She nodded toward the distaff, which Clotho had already

begun to wrap with the raw sheep's wool she'd taken from Arachne's shop.

Atropos nodded approvingly. "Very nice. Where'd you find such good, clean-combed quality?"

Clotho glanced down at the wool, feeling a little guilty for not telling them about visiting Arachne's shop. Then her back straightened. Why should she feel guilty? After all, her sisters had never told her about their trips to the Immortal Marketplace for mail. So she didn't need to tell them about hers!

Lachesis's eyes moved to Clotho's open bag. "Hey, how come your bag is so empty? Where's the rest of your stuff?"

"Oh! Um . . ." Clotho scrambled to come up with an explanation. "It was getting too heavy, so I left some of it in a, uh, safe place about halfway between

Mount Olympus and Earth. Same place I found the wool." That wasn't actually a lie, because the IM *was* halfway between Mount Olympus and Earth.

Luckily, before her sisters could get any nosier, the glowing Destiny List magically appeared, requiring them all to get to work. "C'mon, it's NF time!" said Lachesis. Meaning it was time to assign newborn fates to the many mortal babies who awaited them.

Clotho quickly read the name and description of the first mortal on the list. While she dangled her spindle from one hand, the fingers of her opposite hand set it to twirling clockwise. The fluffy wool on the distaff began to twist into a fine thread, which then wrapped itself around the spindle. *Spin!*

Lachesis stretched out the Thread of Fate to its proper length. *Measure!*

Atropos cut it with careful accuracy. *Snip!*

As the sisters worked, Clotho silently debated whether or not to tell Zeus tomorrow that she'd broken two of his rules. Which would he be angrier over? Her Meleager mistake? Or the fact that she'd hung out with mortals today? *Hmm.* Maybe she should just keep quiet and hope that he never found out about either one.

"Watch out—you almost tangled that thread," Atropos warned suddenly.

Clotho paled, her attention jerking back to her task. "Oh! Sorry! Thanks." She'd better quit daydreaming and focus on her work. She certainly didn't want to make another Meleager-type booboo! Just then, the fortune the Oracle-O cookie from Cassandra's bakery had spoken popped into her head: *Oh, what a tangled web you'll weave, when first you practice to deceive.*

She gulped. Wasn't she deceiving her sisters by not telling them what had happened today and twelve years in the past? And by not letting them know about Zeus's invitation?

Of course she was! Admittedly, she was trying to shield herself from their disapproval. But she was also trying to protect *them* from Zeus's wrath. *Argh!* Just like the Oracle-O cookie had predicted, things were getting more and more tangled. The problem was figuring out how to *un*tangle them!

By the time the sky began to grow pink with the coming of dawn, Clotho still hadn't decided if she should confess her misdeeds to Zeus at his party.

"So where are we meeting next?" Lachesis asked Atropos at the end of their working night.

"Top of the Parthenon?" Atropos suggested. That was one of Athena's most famous Greek temples.

"Okay," agreed Lachesis.

Clotho nodded. "Sure." The night after their night at the Parthenon, their working place would be *her* choice. If only she dared, she might suggest meeting at Arachne's Sewing Supplies at the IM. To her mind, that was an idea almost as bright as Orion's stars!

11

Party Time

WHEN CLOTHO ARRIVED AT ARACHNE'S SHOP the next morning, she tossed the puppets everyone had made into a basket. She also added two new blue-caped serpent puppets she'd found time to knit as Olympian characters that she planned to operate in the show. Then, with Arachne riding on her shoulder, she carried the basket across the atrium to Game On! to meet up with the others.

“Promise you’ll behave at the party?” she asked the spider as they walked through the arched entrance that led into Game On!.

“Yeah, sure,” Arachne said grudgingly. But Clotho noticed she was crossing two of her legs. Was that like crossing fingers behind her back, indicating she didn’t mean what she’d said?

Before Clotho could demand to know, they passed under the second arch and Arachne began clapping those two legs together. “Whoa! Webtastic!” she exclaimed.

Following the spider’s gaze, Clotho felt in awe too. The interior of Game On! looked amazing! In honor of Zeus, its entire balcony had been covered with streamers, balloons, glittery thunderbolts, and other decorations.

His wife, Hera, was rushing around seeing to

last-minute preparations. She was dressed in a long flowing chiton with a gold belt designed to look like a branch of fall leaves, and her hair was fashionably styled high on her head. She looked even more beautiful and statuesque than in paintings Clotho had seen of her.

When Clotho showed up with the finger puppets, Hera oohed and aahed over them, seeming delighted at the prospect of their upcoming performance in honor of Zeus. Yesterday the godboys had painted the large box they'd converted into a puppet theater with images of what they'd referred to as the three *s*s: spears, swords, and statues. Earlier this morning they had moved their theater here.

Since the puppet show was planned as entertainment during the birthday lunch around noon, the five-foot square theater had been placed atop a platform across from a long, fancy table that was already set with gold platters and cutlery. A golden throne—Zeus's seat—was positioned at the table directly opposite the theater so he'd have a prime view. Balloons tied to the back of his chair had the words "Happy Zeus Day" painted on them.

By the time Clotho and the others finished one more practice run of their puppet show, it was almost noon and the party guests had begun to arrive. Aside from the puppeteers, most of the lunch guests were MOA teachers or Zeus's friends like Persephone's mom, Demeter. There were also important mortals like King Menelaus of Sparta, who'd fought in the Trojan War, and King Aeëtes, former owner of the stolen Golden Fleece.

Stomp! Stomp! Stomp! Just then, the birthday guy—Principal Zeus himself—appeared. All eyes turned to where he stood in the archway that led to the balcony, his arms flung wide and a big grin on his face.

"THE BIRTHDAY BOY IS HERE!" he boomed out.

At seven feet tall, Zeus cut an impressive figure with his wild red hair and curly beard, bulging muscles, and piercing blue eyes. Wide, flat gold bracelets encircled his wrists.

A bolt of panic shot through Clotho when she noticed his thunderbolt belt buckle. Would he strike her with an actual thunderbolt if she dared to admit her Meleager mistake or asked him to bend some of his rules for her and her sisters in the future?

On the other hand, he was obviously in a great mood. Probably the best mood she could ever hope to catch him in. So maybe confessing her misdeeds and asking forgiveness sometime today would be a now-or-never chance!

Zeus's eyes lit up when he spied the magnificent birthday cake in the middle of the super-long banquet table. It was shaped like a ten-foot-long thunderbolt and covered with sparkly gold icing. The words "Happy Birthday, King of the Gods and Ruler of the Heavens!" were written in fancy loopy lettering along its length. He licked his lips, rubbed his hands together, and took a step toward it, looking ready to dig in.

Hera rushed over and gave him a big hug. "That's for later," she told him. "Games first. Presents next. Then lunch with cake and a special show, okay?"

"Oh, all right," said Zeus, sounding a bit disappointed at having to wait for cake. But then he cheered up. "Let the games begin!" he bellowed.

With that he and his guests went down to one of the arenas, where they began playing the Calydonian Boar Hunt game. Zeus laughed like crazy when the boar roared down from the mountain. There were no teams this time. It was every immortal for herself or himself.

Clotho giggled to see grown-ups bouncing on trampolines and tossing hilarious statements at one another like "I'm gonna splat you, sucker!" and "You wish!" and "Look out! Zeus on the loose!"

It was especially funny to see the surprised looks on their faces when they realized they'd gotten three strikes out. And even more hilarious when the floor opened up beneath them and the startled players were whisked out of the game.

After more than an hour of play, there were just three grown-ups left in the arena. Pointing to

each one in turn, Athena told Clotho, "Mr. Cyclops is the guy with one eye. He teaches an awesome class at MOA called Hero-ology. That woman is Ms. Nemesis. She teaches Revenge-ology." Then she pointed to her dad. Grinning, she finished, "And you already know who that is!"

"Um, yeah, who doesn't?" said Clotho, grinning back.

Given his strength and size (not to mention his cunning), it was no surprise when Zeus won in the end. On the other hand, no one had tried that hard to splat him out. It was his birthday, after all, and they wanted him to have fun!

He was so thrilled at being the last god standing that he did a happy dance on the floor of the arena. The boom-boom beat of his steps caused the props in the arena to bounce around, which made everyone laugh and cheer.

After that first game, he and the other grown-up immortals tested out some of the punishments in the Tartarus Two game Persephone and Hades had created. These mimicked punishments given out in the real Tartarus in the Underworld, but were more lighthearted. Zeus had no trouble pushing an enormous boulder up a hill in the Sisyphus test, but even he was unable to make it stay put. In another test of skill, players were required to fill a large brass tub with water. But it had so many holes, this proved impossible, and everyone wound up laughing.

Persephone's mom, Demeter, gave her a hug and complimented her and Hades for their work on the game. *Aww, how sweet,* thought Clotho.

When the games were over, Persephone and Hades remained behind at the Tartarus Two game to fix a leak that had sprung up in their lava river before it could cause a flood. They waved the other partygoers off, saying they had it covered.

Everyone else soon gathered around the extra-large table for lunch. Zeus sat dead center in front of the cake, with Hera on one side and Athena on the other. Next to Athena sat Aphrodite, then Artemis. Demeter sat by Hera.

Before sitting down, Clotho set Arachne loose on a nearby wall. "It's for your own safety. You can still watch the festivities from here," she informed the spider when Arachne protested. Truth was, it had occurred to Clotho that some guests might not appreciate a spider hanging around with them at lunch. Plus, she was seated next to Medusa and remembered how her snakes had gotten overly excited when they spotted Arachne in the shop yesterday.

Just like a little kid, Zeus quickly tore through his gifts, his eyes lighting up at the sight of each one. There were thunderbolt-shaped barbells, tunics with thunderbolt-design embroidery, a pair of flying sandals that did tricks, a Thunderopoly board game, a bobblehead Zeus toy, a new saddle for his winged horse, Pegasus, and much more. (Clotho and the other students planned to present all of their puppets to him later.)

As soon as the final gift had been opened, a lavish lunch was served with all of Zeus's favorite foods. There were fancy bowls of yambrosia (a magical, yummy dish whose main ingredients were yams and ambrosia); Underworld stew flavored with asphodel; nectaroni and cheese; celestial soup with noodles shaped like planets and stars; yogurt with pomegranola; and ambrosia salad.

Everyone raised glasses of nectar punch to cheer for Zeus's continued good health.

"This is delicious," Aphrodite said, fluffing her golden hair with one hand as she put her goblet to her lips and took a long sip of the sparkling punch. With that very first sip, her skin began to shimmer more brightly, like it had been dusted with a fine golden glitter. As other immortals drank, the same happened to them—all except for Clotho, of course.

Once all the party guests had eaten their fill, they gathered around to enjoy Apollo's band playing the "Happy Birthday" song. Athena and Hera lit candles on the thunderbolt cake. Zeus made a wish out loud (which was that he'd get the biggest piece of cake). Afterward, he blew out his candles with one humongous puff of breath, which was so strong it ruffled the hair of everyone seated around the table.

When the cake was served, Zeus naturally got his wish. "Yum. This is the best!" he exclaimed, after forking up the first bite of his gigantic slice. Everyone else dug in too.

Ares, Apollo, Poseidon, Athena, Aphrodite, Medusa, Tantalus, and Clotho finished their cake quickly, then gathered at the puppet theater they'd set up. They kneeled behind it in a tight group, puppets on their fingers and their hands held high enough to be seen onstage, while keeping their heads low so their faces would remain hidden.

"Where's Pelops?" Clotho asked Tantalus when it was almost time to begin the performance. She'd noticed that his green-caped puppet wasn't on his finger. Everyone except him was going to wield two puppets or more, since they had twenty-four (a dozen Olympians plus a dozen Titans).

His eyes went shifty. "Oh, I lost him. Doesn't matter. He was just for fun, not really part of the show. I can still narrate without him."

It was true that Pelops wasn't intended to be part of the action, but Clotho was surprised that Tantalus wasn't more upset about losing his puppet. He'd seemed really excited about making it yesterday.

But there was no more time to ponder this. Why? Because it was showtime!

12

Puppets

MOMENTS LATER, TANTALUS ANNOUNCED, "Tonight we present for your entertainment a rollicking reenactment of the Titanomachy. Also known as the Olympian versus Titan War!"

He then launched into his narration. "Thunder-Zeus and his Olympian pals are just minding their own business," he told their audience as Clotho and the others calmly walked their Olympian finger puppets back and forth along the edge of the theater stage.

"Look out! Here comes big bad Crabby-Cronus. This scaredy-crab Titan ruler is afraid the Olympians will grow up to overthrow him. So what does he do? It's horrible. Just watch!" Tantalus went on.

Everyone at the table laughed at the slurping, crunching sounds Medusa made as her crab-shaped Cronus puppet proceeded to gobble as many Olympians as he could. (Because that was what the real Cronus had done in hopes he could stop an Olympian immortal from overthrowing him!)

Later in the show, the guests laughed even louder when Medusa's Cronus puppet was tricked into barfing up those Olympians he'd gobbled down. To show this, the puppeteers tossed their puppets a couple of feet in the air, then let them fall down to the stage floor.

Zeus got so into their antics that he stood up from the table at that point and punched an encouraging fist in the air. "Rally, fellow Olympians, and declare war on the Titans!"

The Olympian puppets did just that. "After ten years of fighting, the puppet Thunder-Zeus gets an idea from an oracle," Tantalus narrated. "Thunder-Zeus invites Mr. Cyclops and his hundred-armed brothers and sisters to help fight the Titans."

Clotho grinned at the obvious delight Ares, Apollo, and Poseidon took in tossing red-yarn bits of fake blood around on the puppet stage during a very silly battle. (The actual battle had been terrible, but this pretend one was lighthearted and meant to amuse the lunch guests.) There were pratfalls, funny voices, and goofy stunts galore. Hearty laughter and cheers rang out at all the silliness.

Just as the Olympian finger puppets were about to win the war, Demeter jumped up from the lunch table and gave a shriek. "Eek! What's this in my cake?" she exclaimed, putting her fingers to her mouth.

The puppet show came to an abrupt halt as everyone's attention fixed on her. They watched Demeter open her mouth and pull out a gooey lump, which she then set on her plate. Even though it was covered in cake frosting, Clotho recognized what it was.

"It's one of our puppets!" yelled Artemis.

Shouts of astonishment were heard. "Ew!" "Yuck!" "What's going on?"

"How did a puppet get in my birthday cake?" Zeus demanded to know.

No one had an answer for that.

Demeter coughed. "I think I swallowed a piece of it. I was so busy watching the show that I didn't

notice what I was eating." Sure enough, a few pieces of yarn were missing from the puppet's shoulder, Clotho saw.

"That's Pelops! Tantalus's puppet. It's wearing a green cape, see?" exclaimed Apollo, pointing at the evidence on Demeter's plate.

"And exactly who is Tantalus?" Zeus roared. It dawned on Clotho just then that Tantalus probably hadn't been officially invited to this party. He'd just sort of invited himself as they were creating the puppet show yesterday.

"Heh-heh." Unfortunately, the mortal boy snickered at that very moment, drawing attention to himself. Carrying something Clotho couldn't see clearly, he was creeping away toward the exit.

Bits of angry electricity zapped from Zeus's muscular arms as he leaped up from his throne.

"You think this is funny, mortal?" he boomed out. He banged his fist so hard on the table that all the plates and cutlery rattled. His eyes narrowed as he demanded, "What have you got behind your back?"

Tantalus froze in his tracks. Slowly and reluctantly, he raised his hands to show what he held—a flask of nectar in one hand and a bag of ambrosia in the other. Gasps sounded.

"You dare to steal the food of the gods?" bellowed Zeus, planting both fists on his hips. "What were you planning to do with those?"

Good question, thought Clotho.

Though he was shaking with fear now, Tantalus stuck out his chin rebelliously. "I was going to Earth to share this stuff with other mortals! Along with the news that immortals can and do make mistakes. And they can be tricked!"

Clotho gasped when he said this. If he was referring to her Meleager mistake, he didn't bring it up right then, however. Instead he said, "I just now tricked the goddess Demeter into eating a bit of my puppet. I mean, funny, right?" His smile fell when no one laughed. Did he really expect them to?

Zeus's eyebrows slammed together in anger. "You have offended and insulted all immortals with your rude trick. You could have made Demeter choke! On top of all that, you attempted to steal food and drink meant only for us immortals!"

"It's not fair that we mortals are denied immortality," Tantalus shot back. "We should get to share the nectar and ambrosia that allow you to live forever!"

More gasps and murmurs ran through the room. "How dare he argue with the King of the Gods!"

"That mortal boy is too bold!" "Uh-oh, Zeus is not going to put up with that!"

Medusa rolled her eyes at Tantalus. "Hate to tell you this, goofball, but nectar and ambrosia don't work on us mortals. Duh. If they did I'd already have used them to turn myself into an immortal, so I could do magic like my two goddessgirl sisters."

"Oh." Tantalus's shoulders slumped at this information.

Suddenly Clotho recalled what her sister Lachesis had said twelve long years ago as she'd watched this boy's Thread of Fate rise toward the heavens. "Looks like Tantalus will enjoy a mostly happy life," she had murmured.

What went wrong? What had brought him to this terrible moment? she wondered.

Then her breath caught in her throat. Could this be

her fault for tangling his thread with Meleager's? Had some of Meleager's unfortunate destiny rubbed off on Tantalus, and Tantalus's fortunate one on Meleager?

While Meleager's life had been extended because of her boo-boo, Tantalus's life seemed about to be cut short. Or at least made unhappier than it might have been. She had to fix things. But how?

Tantalus thrust out his chin. "Immortals do make mistakes, though," he insisted foolishly. "You all saw how I tricked Demeter. And just ask that Fate about Meleager!"

Clotho stiffened when his finger pointed her way. *Gulp.* Seemed he wasn't going to give her a free pass after all. Zeus turned his gaze on her. "Ah, yes. *Meleager.* The log burning in the fireplace. When it turned to ashes, his Thread of Fate was supposed to end. Yet it did not."

"H-how did you know about th-that?" stuttered Clotho.

"I'm the King of the Gods! I know everything," thundered Zeus. From the corner of her eye, Clotho caught a glimpse of Tantalus trying to sneak away again.

Zeus saw him too, and swung his head back toward the boy. "Stop right there!" he commanded. "As I said, you have offended the gods! Do you know what happens to mortals who do that?"

"Uh-oh, here we go," Arachne squeaked, rolling all eight of her eyes. Surprised, Clotho turned her head to see the spider drop from a long silky strand hanging from the ceiling onto her shoulder. Luckily, her voice was so small that only Clotho heard it. And Medusa's snakes were curled close to her head, napping in spite of all the commotion.

Zeus's piercing blue gaze bore into Tantalus. "I hope you enjoy your new home in Tartarus!" he exclaimed. Of course, Tartarus wasn't a place anyone enjoyed being, so Zeus was only being sarcastic.

Finally Tantalus showed the good sense to become truly terrified. Trembling, he dropped to his knees and begged for mercy. "P-please, spare me! I wasn't thinking. My thoughts got t-tangled up." Then, to Demeter, he added, "I'm sorry."

Taking pity on the foolish mortal, Demeter said to Zeus, "No need to be too harsh. I wasn't done any permanent harm."

Hera nodded, her voice soft as she put a gentle hand on Zeus's arm. "He's just a boy. And he didn't succeed in sharing the nectar and ambrosia with other mortals."

This seemed to calm Zeus somewhat, but he

didn't back down entirely, probably fearing that if he did so, other mortals would hear of it and think him weak. "All right," he said. "I'll come up with another punishment, then. Let's see, what will fit his crime?"

"Remember how you punished the Titan Prometheus?" nudged Athena. "That seemed fair."

When Arachne muttered, "Again with the punishments," Clotho shushed her. Honestly, someone was going to smush that spider one of these days if she didn't behave!

Now Aphrodite spoke up too. "What Tantalus tried to do *is* kind of similar. He wanted ambrosia and nectar to help mortals. When Prometheus set the Hero-ology classroom on fire at MOA, it was a misguided effort to help mortals on Earth obtain the gift of fire."

"Right! So for Prometheus's punishment I

decided that every time he took a bite of liver—his least favorite food—more liver would magically appear on his plate. *Whoa!* That was a good one, if I do say so myself. And I do!" Zeus cracked up, delighted and impressed by his own cleverness.

Just then Clotho had a thought that might save Tantalus but still please Zeus. "What if whatever punishment you decide on for Tantalus takes place here in Game On!" she suggested. "It could be carried out in the new Tartarus Two game instead of in the actual Tartarus in the real Underworld, which would be way harsher, I'm guessing."

"You got that right," Persephone mumbled. She and Hades had just arrived, apparently having fixed their game's bathtub leak.

"Perfect!" roared Zeus. Latching onto Clotho's idea, he pointed a finger at Tantalus. "I sentence

you to report here to Game On! after school every day for the next month."

A smile broke out on Tantalus's face and he jumped to his feet. "That's my punishment? To play a game here every day for a month? Awesome!"

"Not so awesome," Zeus corrected him. "You will play a game all right, but you will lose every time."

"Huh?" Tantalus's face crumpled in disappointment.

Just when Clotho began to hope that Zeus might forget about her mistake with Meleager, her sisters walked in. *Oh no!*

"Are we late? What did we miss? We just happened to run across a magic breeze and learn we were invited to Zeus's birthday party today," said Lachesis.

Atropos glanced toward Clotho. "Why didn't you

tell us about the invitation? The breeze said it had been delivered to you."

"Oh really?" Zeus caught Clotho's guilty expression and raised an eyebrow. "Party's over!" he announced abruptly. "Hera, please shoo everybody out except the three Fates. I want to have a private talk with them."

"Well, that party was kind of a bust. Not even one fly showed up!" grumbled Arachne as everyone but Zeus, the Fates, and her departed.

When Clotho just groaned, Arachne added, "What? Are you stressing? Don't worry. Even if Zeus decides to turn you into a spider as punishment, at least you'll still be immortal."

"Great," Clotho whispered back. "Not!"

13
Amazing Arachne

ONCE THE OTHER PARTY GUESTS HAD GONE, Zeus turned to the three Fates. "Do you know how close we came to real trouble just now? If mortals come to believe that immortals make mistakes just like they do, they'll lose respect for us. That's why I make rules, to avoid that kind of misunderstanding. Yet you broke them. Explain yourselves!"

"Huh?" said Lachesis.

"I don't understand," said Atropos. With confusion and suspicion in their eyes, both sisters turned to stare at Clotho.

"I'm sorry," Clotho told them. "This is all my fault." She looked at Zeus. "I didn't mean to mingle with mortals." She went on to explain how she'd broken Rule #3 yesterday. Then she told of the tangled web of deceit she'd begun to weave twelve years ago. How she'd failed to admit she'd tangled Meleager's thread, and that his thread had brushed Tantalus's as their two threads floated heavenward.

Gathering her courage, she said to Zeus, "I hope you can forgive my mistake. But about Rule Number Three—"

"'But'?" Zeus roared, crossing his strong arms over his chest. "There are no 'buts.' My rules are ironclad. And you must obey them!"

Clotho flinched. But instead of backing down, which probably would have been the smart thing to do, she tried again. "The thing is, mortals don't like the Fates. I hoped that if they got to know us, they'd see we aren't so bad. But the only way for them to get to know us is by breaking your Rule Number Three—by *mingling*."

"Mortals don't like you?" Zeus echoed, uncrossing his arms and appearing shocked. "Well, that's ridiculous. What's not to like?"

"She's right," Lachesis agreed meekly, surprising Clotho with her support. "Mortals think we boss them around and make willy-nilly decisions about their lives. Decisions they sometimes don't like."

Atropos nodded. "They send us angry letters."

"Angry letters?" Zeus boomed, causing all three girls to jump. "Hmm, that's not good. I mean,

they don't need to be your best friends, but they shouldn't dislike you either. You do them a service. Left to their own devices, without destiny providing a path for their lives, they'd make way more bad decisions than they already do. We need to fix this. But how?" Deep in thought, he stroked the tip of his curly red beard as he paced around the balcony. *Stomp. Stomp. Stomp.*

The sisters watched him for a while. Then Clotho boldly piped up again. "What if the Threads of Fate we spin, measure, and cut didn't impose an absolute life limit or life path? Maybe instead the threads' predictions could be changed through a mortal's wise decisions? So that their destinies aren't so fixed."

Atropos cocked her head, looking intrigued. "I get it. So if a mortal uses good sense and works hard to make good choices in life that we Fates didn't anticipate, they might live longer and more happily than their threads predicted?"

Clotho nodded.

Lachesis looked between the two of them, her eyes sparkling as she caught on. "That would mean they might even accomplish things that were not a known part of their destiny at birth. How exciting!"

"Could they really do that, though? Sad to say, some mortals are not very bright," mused Zeus.

"Maybe they could. With our help. We could make ourselves more available to them," Clotho suggested tentatively. "And sort of . . . well . . . *coach* them. Encourage them to look for ways to change their lives if they are unhappy with them. If they feel they have some say in their futures, maybe they won't get so mad at us."

"I like it!" said Lachesis.

"But where would we meet them?" wondered Atropos. "We have no fixed address!"

"Ooh! Ooh! Idea alert!" squeaked a small voice. *Arachne,* of course. Clotho groaned softly as Zeus and her sisters startled. Their heads turned this way and that as they searched for the owner of the voice.

Clotho pointed to her shoulder. "Um . . . that was my, uh, *friend* Arachne speaking."

"Arachne? The woman my Theeny bested in that weaving contest and then turned into a spider?" bellowed Zeus.

"Hello? Do you think that just because spiders don't have ears, I can't hear you unless you shout?" Arachne informed him. "Just so you know, these legs of mine are not just pretty. The hairs on them detect sound!" As usual she couldn't (or maybe *wouldn't*) put the brakes on her mouth even in the presence of immortals. Including the King of the Gods!

Zeus scowled. "I remember you, all right. You dared to insult the gods with your rude weavings! You even made fun of *me*!"

"Yeah, yeah. Water under the bridge," scoffed Arachne, shrugging yet again. Then to the three Fates she said, "Truth is, I get kind of lonely in my shop. If you'd agree to help me run it, I'd love to see it humming with customers again. You could meet and chat with mortals there."

A smile blossomed inside Clotho at the little spider's words. Arachne might be quick tempered and too blunt for her own good, but one had to admire her spunk! She just hoped that that spunk wouldn't get Arachne in trouble again. What would Zeus think of her suggestion?

After a few more moments of pacing, he halted

and held up a finger. "I just got an amazing idea," he announced to Clotho and her two sisters. "How about if I tweak my rules a bit so that mortals are still assigned destinies, but they are allowed to overcome certain negative aspects in their destinies through smart choices and good decisions? And maybe they could meet with you occasionally at the IM for guidance. Maybe at that sewing shop that closed down."

At this, Arachne was speechless for once, while the three sisters looked at one another with raised brows. Because Zeus had just suggested the very same things they and Arachne had come up with, only in his own words. Still, everyone knew Zeus liked to be the best at everything, especially at coming up with ideas. So, wisely, they all agreed with him.

"Excellent idea. And the meeting place is perfect.

Halfway between the Earth and Mount Olympus!" said Clotho.

Atropos and Lachesis nodded energetically.

"Great!" boomed Zeus, gazing at each Fate in turn. "I order you to get started on my new plan right away!" With that he grabbed a plate holding another large piece of his thunderbolt cake, and headed out of Game On!

Eyes twinkling, Clotho turned to her sisters and clapped her hands together in glee. "Arachne's shop is really cool. Come have a look. It's right across the atrium."

In minutes they were all pushing inside Arachne's Sewing Supplies. Right away Lachesis spotted the huge loom in one corner of the shop. She squealed in delight.

"Here, I'll help you string it," offered Clotho.

Once it was strung, Lachesis eagerly set to work, passing new threads over and under, and then pulling the threads tight at the end of each row.

Meanwhile, Atropos had wandered over to explore the craft section, eyeing with interest all the scissors and shears. Clotho left Lachesis at the loom and sidled up to Atropos. "Maybe you could teach art classes in paper cutting," Clotho suggested slyly. "I bet mortals would *love* that!" Atropos's face lit with excitement.

To both sisters Clotho said, "During the daytime we could take turns counseling mortals who need our guidance regarding their destinies. Whoever isn't counseling could help run the shop with Arachne. What do you think?"

She held her breath as she waited for her sisters to shoot down her ideas. But to her astonishment, that didn't happen for once.

Meow!

"Oh! Look—how cute," said Lachesis as the shop kitten wandered in. She picked it up and held it, stroking a gentle hand over its soft white fur.

"Yeah, bonus! We could keep this kitten for our pet if we hang out here," Clotho added quickly.

"Come look upstairs!" Arachne's little voice called out. She leaped onto Clotho's shoulder once more as they all went up. Together, the spider and Clotho showed Lachesis and Atropos how, since there were three empty rooms upstairs, each of the sisters could have her very own private space.

"Meeting mortals here during the daytime is one thing. But actually making this place our home?" Lachesis said thoughtfully. "I don't know."

"Yeah. Nomads no more? That's a big step," Atropos mused. "I'm not sure."

"Oh, stop it," grumped Arachne. "Just think of my shop as a place to stash your stuff, work, do crafts, and hang out. It's not like you're chained here and can never go anywhere else. A little spider like me can't travel as easily as you on a whim. Count yourselves lucky!"

Though Clotho agreed with what the spider had said, she figured her sisters would respond better to persuasion than to grumpiness. "If we have a home of our own, it'll be easier to keep track of our stuff," she said. "And wouldn't it be awesome not to have to drag all of it with us everywhere we go?" This was an argument she thought might appeal to her sisters, though it wasn't the main reason she wanted to move in here.

Finally, for what seemed like the millionth, possibly billionth, time, Clotho asked them the question that revealed her deepest desire. "Wouldn't it be great to have our own home? A place we truly belonged?" Taking a big breath, she braced herself for disappointment. For them to say no as usual.

Only, this time, her sisters surprised her. "Maybe . . . ," mused Lachesis.

"Possibly . . . ," pondered Atropos.

Then: "Yeah, let's try it," her two sisters said at the same time.

A grin spread over Clotho's face. *Woo-hoo!*

14
Tantalize

CLICK CLACK CLICK CLACK WENT CLOTHO'S knitting needles. It was the following Friday, and she was sitting in a comfy chair knitting a family of merpeople for a mermaid friend of Poseidon's named Amphitrite. Pausing, she gazed around Arachne's shop—her cozy new home. The green-eyed shop kitten, which she and her sisters had named Destiny, was playing with a ball of orange yarn at her feet.

After doing their official jobs here each night for the past week, the Fates had then spent their days cleaning the sewing shop from top to bottom. The paper covering the windows was gone and so was all the dust, making everything much cheerier. Bolts of cloth now stood straight upon the shelves, and balls of yarn were neatly displayed according to color in various baskets and cubbies.

Using the shop's loom, Lachesis had woven a large, new sign they'd hung out front. It read:

Arachne's Sewing Supplies

(and Home of the Fates)

Clotho had finished her green serpent puppet family earlier. Tonight they planned to work in the land of the Amazon women, which was near Colchis.

So it would be easy for her to drop the new green puppets off for the lonely serpent that lurked under the tree. She hoped the creature would enjoy them. Perhaps having them around would improve its disposition, even if they were only puppets. Because Arachne, Destiny the kitten, and the Colchis serpent had made her realize that immortals and mortals weren't the only ones who sometimes got lonely. Creatures did too. *Everybody* needed friends.

Lifting her gaze from her craftwork briefly, she spotted Arachne. High in the shop's corners, the spider was busily spinning new sayings in her webs. Gone were the insults. From now on, she'd promised her webs would only contain perky announcements such as SALE ON KNIT KITS AND RED THREAD and REGISTER FOR DATES TO MEET THE FATES and SIGN UP FOR WEAVING AND PAPER-CUTTING LESSONS!

Turned out, Arachne had a talent for advertising.

Clotho turned her gaze on Lachesis. At this very moment she was happily weaving fabric for a wedding dress that Hera had designed for a bride-to-be who'd ordered it at her shop. And Atropos was contentedly cutting out snowflake garlands for a display Cassandra had requested to decorate her family's bakery.

Jingle-jangle! The bell they'd hung on the sewing-shop door alerted them to a new arrival. It was Hermes, coming by to deliver their mail.

"Hey, new neighbors! Welcome to the IM!" he called, dropping a large box just inside the door. After he departed, Clotho eyed the box like it was stinky bird poop. Would the letterscrolls inside be filled with rude complaints and cruel criticisms from mortals? It took all her courage to sort through and read them with her sisters.

To her surprise, though there were mean letter-scrolls among them, far more were kind. Some even contained praise and thanks for the work she and her sisters did.

There were also helpful suggestions. Like that the Fates should write a column in *Teen Scrollazine* with advice on how to improve one's destiny. Cool! Maybe one day soon she'd go talk to the scrollazine's editors about this idea! There were also requests for one-on-one meetings in the shop in the upcoming weeks, and suggestions for future craft-class offerings. All of this gave her hope that someday mortals would see the Fates in a better (or maybe *good*) light. Not as enemies to be feared.

Later that afternoon when the shop bell jangled, Medusa leaned inside. Propping the door open with one foot, she waved Clotho and her sisters over. "You've got to come see what's going on at Game On!" she called out.

The Fates glanced at one another, then jumped up and followed the snake-haired girl across the atrium. As they entered the Game On! balcony and went to stand at its railing, they saw that the new Tartarus Two game was in progress down in the arena. Athena and others had already gathered to watch.

Atropos elbowed Clotho. "Look! Tantalus is one of the players!"

"He can only score points to move ahead in the game if he can grab snacks and drinks," Athena informed them.

"He doesn't look too happy," noted Clotho. While the others playing the game seemed to be having a good time, he obviously was *not*. He frowned with

frustration as he stood knee-high in a pool of water beneath a fruit tree with low-hanging branches. Whenever he reached for the fruit, the branches jerked away from his grasp. If he bent for a drink of water, the water drained away before he could get even a sip. It was impossible for him to score.

"Zeus named this feature 'Tantalize,'" Medusa told them.

"He purposely based the word on Tantalus's name," Athena added. "Dad hopes that even after Tantalus's punishment ends, mortals will always remember his fate. It will serve as a warning of what can happen when one offends the gods."

"This punishment stinks!" Tantalus yelled, stomping a foot in the pool and splashing himself in the process.

"Poor Tantalus." Clotho couldn't help feeling a

little sorry for him. Not only did he have to endure four weeks of this frustration, he also had to endure the teasing of the other players.

"Serves you right, Ambrosia Boy!" Ares mocked.

"Yeah, Nectar Nose!" Apollo hooted. Then the two godboys successfully played through a far more entertaining punishment nearby involving grabbing dangling vines to swing over a steaming pit of lava.

As they moved on to enjoy another part of the game, Tantalus sighed and scowled after them. "Rub it in, why don't you? I can't believe I'm stuck having to come here and do this after school *every day* for a whole month! Guess it could be worse, though." He snatched at the branches again, never catching hold of the tempting fruit dangling above his head.

He was so right, thought Clotho. Despite the boy's grumbling, his punishment could've been *much* worse. He was fortunate that Zeus had been convinced not to send him to the *real* Tartarus.

As she and her sisters headed back to Arachne's shop, she reflected on how very lucky they were that Zeus had "adopted" their ideas. Letting them tweak the absoluteness of mortal fate and also mix with mortals to bring about friendlier relations was *big*!

Pride surged through Clotho when she thought about how, instead of accepting *her* fate, she'd used all her powers of persuasion to convince Zeus to alter some of his rules for the good of both mortals *and* the Fates. As a result, she now had a pet and a home. And all the time in the world to work on her beloved knitting projects.

Plus, lots of new friends had begun popping into the shop to chat or get crafty advice. Just this morning, for example, Atalanta had come by. She'd invited

Clotho to be on her team in a new Argonaut-themed game in Game On! that would open later today. And yesterday Cassandra had asked for her help in writing some fortunes for her Opposite Oracle-O cookies. Clotho wasn't the only one with new friends either. Athena had surprised and pleased Arachne the other day by asking for her advice on a new weaving she was doing.

Clotho sighed, a soft smile curving her lips. Her new life was a dream come true. Surrounded by friends, her sisters, a pet, work she enjoyed, plus yarn and other crafty stuff, Clotho wasn't lonely anymore. She was something else.

Happy.